Before
Cursed Beast

The *Before* Series
Book 3

by
Michelle Deerwester-Dalrymple

Before the Cursed Beast

Copyright 2022 Michelle Deerwester-Dalrymple All rights reserved
ISBN: 9798439312252
Imprint: Independently published

Edited by Phoenix Promo
Chapter art licensed by vukoble through Depositphotos
Cover art licensed through Canva.com

All rights reserved. In accordance with the U.S. Copyright Act of 1976, the scanning, uploading, distribution, or electronic sharing of any part of this book without the permission of the author constitutes unlawful piracy of the author's intellectual property. If you would like to use the material from this book, other than for review purposes, prior authorization from the author must be obtained. Copies of this text can be made for personal use only. No mass distribution of copies of this text is permitted.

This book is a work of fiction. Names, dates, places, and events are products of the author's imagination or used factiously. Any similarity or resemblance to any person living or dead, place, or event is purely coincidental.

Before the Cursed Beast

Author's Note:

My two favorite fairy tales are *Cinderella and Beauty and the Beast*. My first book, *Before the Glass Slipper*, was my retelling of *Cinderella*. This one is my *Beauty and the Beast* retelling, and it is one of my favorite books to date.

This book is not a traditional romance. Instead of steamy romance, these fairy tale reads are a bit darker and follows the depths of humanity in the lives of our favorite villains and characters before their infamous stories. Please be ready for something a bit darker, not steamy, and perhaps not the happy, fairy tale ending we are used to!

If you love this book, be sure to leave a review! Reviews are life blood for authors, and I appreciate every review I receive!

Love what you read? Want more from Michelle? **Click the image below to receive Gavin, the free Glen Highland Romance short FREE ebook and The Heartbreak of the Glen FREE ebook,** book sales and promotions, updates, and more in your inbox.

Get your free copy by signing up for my newsletter at linktr.ee/mddalrympleauthor

Before the Cursed Beast

Table of Contents

Chapter One	7
Chapter Two	16
Chapter Three	25
Chapter Four	34
Chapter Five	45
Chapter Six	55
Chapter Seven	64
Chapter Eight	73
Chapter Nine	88
Chapter Ten	101
Chapter Eleven	118
Chapter Twelve	129
Chapter Thirteen	142
Chapter Fourteen	152
Chapter Fifteen	165
Chapter Sixteen	174
Chapter Seventeen	193
Fairy Tale Notes	209
A Thank You–	211
About the Author	212
Also by the Author:	214

Before the Cursed Beast

Before the Cursed Beast

*Sometimes our fairy tale ending is
of our own making*

Before the Cursed Beast

Chapter One

I rushed into the magician's study, my skirts whipping at my legs, my arms full of clay jars, and my heart full of fear.

It hadn't always been this way, with fear ruling my life. Years ago, when I was a girl, the magician had seemed like a guardian, a caring protector. He was my first love, my first kiss, my first role model. But once I started to learn magic and master it with skill, he had changed. No longer did I play with childish magic, training rodents as pets or opening flowers in a field. *Non*, real magic affected the hearts and minds of people, and

Adolphe's behavior towards me changed as quickly as if I'd cast a spell on him.

When he used to speak to me with kind words, he now barked demands and insults. Where we had once worked side by side, he now banished me from the study and relegated me to demeaning cleaning and gathering chores. When once he had touched me with love and adoration, he now delivered his harsh words with a smack or a slap.

And I was disappearing.

Not really, not like magical disappearing where something is no longer present at all. *Non*, disappearing into myself, losing what I used to be, a cherubic girl who loved to play with her guardian and magic.

Now every aspect of magic frightened me, or worried me, as I waited for a curse or a heavy hand. I no longer smiled, and my once-shiny chestnut hair had become ashen, stringy. I had taken to sleeping in the kitchens, as I didn't want Adolphe to find me.

And it suited. I was treated as nothing more than a servant in what had once been my home. Why not sleep where the servants do?

"Salome! Where are you with my concoctions? Even a fool could work faster than you!"

Adolphe's harsh words exploded from his darkened study and carried into the hall where I juggled the jars. I held my breath as I walked, afraid of what he might do if I dropped a jar, or even almost dropped one . . .

I rushed into the study and placed the jars on his disheveled worktable. Gone were the days where I perched on the table and watched him work. Now I cowered behind it.

"Took you long enough," Adolph threw over his shoulder at me.

He faced his bookshelf, lifting the lids off glass jars and sniffing. Though his study was large, with vaulted ceilings reinforced with wood beams and a single long window at the far side of the room, Adolphe still took up so much space. He was tall, taller than most other men I'd met, limited though that might be, and his black velveteen cloak added to his dramatic flair. The olive undertone to his skin prevented him from appearing washed out, even in the dim light of the wall sconces.

"I had to find the right jars. There were so many in the cellar –"

"If you paid better attention, then maybe you'd find what you were looking for in a more timely manner." His tone grew more harsh as he spoke.

"I'm sorry, I —"

"I don't want to hear your paltry excuses," Adolphe bit back. "Now put the jars in the center of the table, with the earwig dust closest to me. Then leave and make yourself useful by cleaning the rooms in this tower. You've let it become filthy."

I bowed my head, trying to hide in the folds of my stained gray gown. When was the last time I'd worn a brightly hued gown, or one of rich jeweled tones? Or even a new one? Months? Years? This one lost all its color and barely reached my ankles.

"Yes, Adolphe," I answered, casting my eyes at the floor.

He grumbled to himself as I picked up the jars and moved them as he asked. I had grabbed the last one when it slipped from my shaking fingers onto the table. The jar didn't break, *thank the stars,* I thought in a panic, but the contents – powdered dung from the smell of it – spilled all over the table and his assorted papers and herbs.

My hands froze. Maybe I could clean it up before he saw. Maybe I –

Adolphe stopped his grumbling and whirled around. His black eyes blazed in his face, and I shrunk back from him.

"'Tis only the dung. I can clean it –"

Adolphe's hand slammed onto the table with such force, all the jars clinked on the table, threatening to fall over.

They didn't, and I released a slow, shaky breath. Then I looked up at Adolphe and cowered back more.

"Get you gone from here. You are as useless as a cane for a bird."

I ran. At the door, I tripped over my tangled skirts but didn't pause. Instead, I hiked my skirts to my knees and raced for the sanctuary of the cellar kitchens.

Souris stood at the counter table, slicing rough bread that was assuredly part of our meager dinner. He flipped his graying brown hair from his soft hazel eyes that looked at me with a mix of pity and concern. It was a look I'd grown accustomed to over these past several months. And it made him appear as mousy as the rodent he was named for.

"You made it out without a scratch this time. That pleases my aging heart, Salome."

I stood opposite him at the counter, the dwindling hearth fire at my back, permitting the cool spring air to gain a hold on the cellar.

"His harsh words wound just as deeply." My shoulders sagged over the worn tabletop. "I wish I knew what had changed in him."

The steady movements of Souris's hand were the only movements in the quiet kitchens until the hearth snapped behind us as it fully died down.

Without turning, I extended my hand behind me and twitched my fingers. The fire immediately sprung to life as if given kindling.

Souris's hand froze mid-slice, and he stared straight at me. His mouth dropped open, but several seconds passed before his lips formed any words.

"The fire –" he whispered, pointing at it with a warped, calloused finger.

I flicked my dark locks over my shoulder at the now-flaming hearth. The heat pressed against my face, forcing the chill of the stone kitchens away.

"What about the fire? It was low, and I was cold."

Souris set the knife down, but his eyes were riveted on me. "When did you learn to control fire like that? So easily?"

I glanced at my hand, as if the secret to fire was printed on my fingers. "I don't understand. I've been studying it, and Adolphe had been training me. I've been able to do it for a while. Why wouldn't I learn the power of fire?"

I lifted my gaze back to Souris. Any pity or concern on his face had been erased by wide-eyed surprise.

"You weren't borne to Adolphe. He found you when the travelers left. He was young himself and took you home and loved you. He showed you all the secrets but never expected . . ."

I narrowed my eyes at my dear friend. "Never expected anything from me? He thought only he owned the secrets of the universe?"

"Did he see you light a fire with nothing but a flick of your hand?"

"*Oui*," I admitted, returning my attention to my slender white hand. Who would have thought my tiny hands could hold so much power? The realization of what Souris was saying dawned on me like an ugly sun. Adolphe loved me when he thought I was nothing special and had no power. "Is he? Is he afraid of my skills?"

Souris nodded slowly, as if trying to work it out himself. "*Oui*, of course. It all makes sense."

"But that doesn't make sense!" I whined. "Why would he suddenly hate me because I have the power of fire?"

Souris finally moved. He had set the knife down and reached across the narrow span of the table to grasp my hands. I released a shuddering breath. The touch of another person, so missed these past months, stirred me to my core.

"Adolphe only truly loves himself. He humored you because you didn't have magic, or so he thought. He could show off his. Modesty has never been one of Adolphe's strong points."

I blinked quickly, trying to prevent the flood of tears that threatened to fall. The past several months were starting to make sense in my head, as if the pieces of a torn recipe were knitting together to be legible. I feared if I let the tears fall, then I would lose the sight of my situation that I presently had. And I didn't want Souris to know how badly I ached from Adolphe withdrawing his affections from me.

"You are right," I agreed, nodding my head. "Once he caught me stoking a fire without touching it, he turned from me."

Souris patted my hand. "His loss. You will always have a place here with me. You are the daughter I never had." He lifted a hand and waved it around the room. "And this old tower is falling apart around our ears. The cleaning and repairing is never ending. I would welcome your company in caring for it."

His eyes softened again, and with it, my heart. I may have lost love with Adolphe, at least I still had the fatherly love of Souris. Perhaps I wasn't as unlovable as Adolphe had made me feel as of late.

"*Merci*, Souris. I appreciate you more than you know."

Picking his bread knife up again, he winked at me before cutting another slice. "*Non*, I'm the one who's grateful. Never shall I have to kindle another fire as long as you are with me."

Chapter Two

While it seemed that Adolphe had banished me from his study, my exile didn't last, and soon he had me back in his darkened room, assisting him.

His words didn't soften, however, and neither did his heavy hand. But I was a quick learner, both of his spells and of his behavior. As long as I hid anything I learned or any new magical powers I acquired, he dismissed me as little more than a bothersome fly. And I never used my fire magic in front of him again.

Rather, I kept my eyes wide open, studying everything he did, even if he wasn't teaching me directly. I was determined to learn, to grow, even as

Adolphe worked to keep me in the dark. The light of learning burned deep inside me, and I'd do whatever it took to keep that small flame lit.

Souris cautioned me daily, warning that Adolphe's retribution would be harsh and swift if my subterfuge was discovered, but that didn't stop me from smuggling books from his study under my skirts when I tidied up after Adolphe retired to his chambers for the night. As long as I had the books back in the study before he arrived the next morning, he was none the wiser.

And if he noticed the purple moons under my eyes from lack of sleep, he didn't comment on it. Since I no longer had time during the day to study the precious books, I was forced to read them at night, tucked under a thin blanket in the kitchen near the fire eternally blazing by my hand.

The words on the page were like a drug for me – they came to life, as bright as the fire in the hearth, and blazed their way through my mind, burning in my blood. The spells and potions imprinted in my mind, weaving through me like thread on a loom, to become a part of me.

I often fell asleep on the books, then rushed to replace them on their stands before Adolphe entered in the morn. I was fortunate that Adolphe tended to be a late sleeper, often still pulling his cape on as he walked into his study well after sunrise. He barely glanced at me when he did so and went right to his over-honeyed tea and buttered toast Souris left as a snack.

My larger problem was application. The theory from the books was only as useful as I could practice the skills. Some of the spells involved speaking words and moving my hands – those I could practice on my own time in the kitchens, the barn, or behind the hen house.

The larger spells and the potions, those were another matter altogether. How might I sneak out his black or red candles? He would see they were burned down if I used them. And I couldn't begin considering his jars. While I had access to milk, rose petals, and eggshells, the rarer ingredients, mole grindings or flies' wings, were out of my reach. Adolphe would surely notice those were lower, like the candles. He watched his ingredients like a hawk, always complaining about their expense. When he met with the apothecary for items he couldn't collect himself, the apothecary's hand shook as he measured out and weighted the items under Adolphe's ferocious stare.

It's hopeless, I lamented.

Or so I thought. Until one day when Adolphe's draping sleeve swept over several glass jars, knocking them to the floor, where they shattered. Glass and dust and grindings littered the floor in a sparkling mess.

"*Merde!*" Adolphe screamed, then turned his fury on me. I cowered away, trying to hide behind my stained skirts and wracking my brain for any words that might placate him, keep his fist from landing on my face.

"I'll clean it right away," I promised in a shaky voice.

"See that you do! But now I can't complete my work!" Adolphe swung around, his cape sweeping in a wide circle around the room, disturbing the cache of spilled herbs. I held my breath, waiting for him to knock another jar to the ground that he would blame me for.

"*Oui*," I answered, scrambling out the door to find a broom.

Adolphe strode down the dim, cobwebbed hall to his quarters as I raced for the kitchens to retrieve a broom. When I saw him again, he had the hood to his cape covering his head and his bag in hand.

"See it cleaned before I return. The contents are useless now, tainted by the glass and dirt on the floor. Make sure they are destroyed in the fire." He paused and eyed me up and down. The look on his face sent a slash of chills down my spine. Why was he looking at me like that? "You should be good at that," he added before swirling around and slamming the heavy wooden door as he left.

And with his departure, I also saw opportunity. Without fully thinking on it, I rushed to the kitchens to retrieve several leather bags hanging on pegs. Typically, they were used for storing oat cakes or leftover bread. I had other plans for them.

I crept into Adolphe's study on nervous toes, as if he might catch me even as he was on the road to the village. I still looked over my shoulder, fearing he'd discover me with every step I took. I was fortunate that Adolphe had a hatred for animals. If he owned a cat or a bird familiar, I surely would have believed it was spying on me, ready to report my actions to Adolphe.

Under the shadowy, flickering light of the wall sconces, I bent to the mess. But I didn't sweep it all up. First, I pulled out each piece of glass and set them all in the dustpan. Then, using the side of my hand, I did my best to separate the contents from one another. Some were easy – ground cattails were a dark brown while mole dust was gray, and ground beetles were black. But others, ugh, it just looked like dirt. How could I separate that?

A banging sound from below made me jump, and I glanced around the room. I knew it was too soon for Adolphe to be back, yet I worked quickly, as if he were climbing the stairs behind me. I swept the different piles into their own leather bags and tucked the bags in the loose bodice of my gown.

Working quickly with the rest of the debris, I swept the remnants up and returned to the kitchens, where I tossed the glass and dirt into the fire where it snapped and popped. If Adolphe asked, I could show him the glass remnants, and he'd be assured I had destroyed all the materials.

Once I was done, I finally took a deep breath to calm my quivering insides. While Souris was outside, I tucked the tiny bags under my blanket. I didn't want him to see what I was doing. If Adolphe asked him any questions, Souris could be completely honest in saying he didn't know. I'd never forgive myself if Souris were punished for my actions.

As I put the broom back in its corner, I smiled to myself. Finally, I had some of the more exotic supplies I needed for the spells and potions I'd committed to memory.

It was time to start testing my skills.

Adolphe didn't even glance at me sideways when he returned from his excursion to town. I breathed a heady sigh of relief, but as Souris exited the kitchens to take supper to Adolphe, who had locked himself in his rooms for the night, my chest clenched with a twinge of sadness. I recalled the days when Adolphe would take me with him to the town. We didn't speak to anyone, but I loved investigating the mysteries of the apothecary shop, trailing my fingers over the multi-chromatic jars and bottles, peering into the glass to see bits of fur or dust or feathers. Dried grasses and flowers hung from the ceiling rafters, next to leathery skins or desiccated birds' feet. Every nook and cranny of the shop was an enigma and surprise. Then the apothecary would complement my bright cognac eyes that he said reminded him of his favorite spirit. At the time, his compliment was another mystery to me. What was cognac?

And I didn't ask what cognac meant as I wasn't permitted to speak to anyone – Adolphe preferred privacy in all things. But he always took me to the *patisserie* after the apothecary, where we would sit outside on fine days, drinking hot chocolate and eating buttery croissants that melted in my mouth. I'd take in the views of the village, of women rushing past with their baskets and gossip, of men leading mules and goats and carts, of children playing with hoops or field mice.

And my favorite view, in the distance, shrouded in pinks and purples against the mountain, was the castle itself. I loved to image visiting that regal home, of meeting the old king and queen and their beloved son. While Adolphe had rattled off his irritations about the old king and the prince who would soon take over, about how the king-to-be was a snide, spoiled young man who would ruin the kingdom, I admired the stone monolith sparkling in the sun and dreamed of seeing its colorful windows up-close and investigate the myriad rooms. My imagination had run wild as I licked slick buttery crumbs from my fingertips.

Oh, such were the joys of my childhood, so unlike the dismal present day. I sighed to myself as I watched Souris's tan leather jerkin and trousers disappear up the narrow servant steps of the tower. Perhaps one day I'd have the chance to go to town on my own, enter those stores we had ignored in the past, speak to whomever I desired.

My eyes flashed to my rumpled bedding that hid the leather bags with my newfound treasures.

Maybe that day of going to the village by myself wasn't merely a dream, or as far off as I believed. If I could develop my skills, then I might leave this tower, strike out on my own, sell my spells and potions, and live by myself. I didn't require much. A small hut in the wood might suffice.

And if I got really good, perhaps I'd even find myself on the front steps of the king's castle one day, selling my talents to royalty itself.

A fire ignited inside me like the one I lit in the hearth, one that demanded I move, I practice, I apply what I had been secretly learning, so that those fantasies might one day come true.

Chapter Three

Oh, but the first few times I tried to use the spilled ingredients, I failed horribly.

I used thread and a burnt piece of wood from the fire to mark the leather skins with the contents I was sure of, the cattails and the like. But that pile I swept together, the indiscernible dust that was looking to be a mess. And no matter what I tried, I couldn't separate the dust from the dirt.

I'd have to find a spell or potion that employed the whole set. And then I would have to hope the amounts I used were close to what was required, which was not the best philosophy to apply when developing potions.

The first spell I cast on my first night of experimenting was a hiding spell. Souris had cautioned me about what Adolphe would do if he found out about my improved skill. I shivered at the thought. A hiding spell to secret the leather bags from his awareness was just the thing.

The only spell I could think of was a rite to protect my home. Well, my bedding. I gathered an old, small box and coriander, spoke the words to bind my belongings with iron and chains to keep my sanctuary safe, then emptied the seeds into the box and tucked it next to my shelf. It wasn't much, but it would have to do for now.

Once that was finished, I studied my leather packets and decided to try to dust and dirt mixture. Maybe I could discern the contents and how they could be used if I tried them in a potion.

But what potion? Sitting atop my blankets, I tapped my chin as I stared into the fire. I shifted my gaze around the kitchen, looking for inspiration, when I noticed Souris had left his cutting knife on the table. He had commented that his fingers had been aching lately, especially when it rained, and chilly rain was the worst.

A spell or potion to block that pain would work, and I knew it used mole dust, which was part of the mixture.

Nothing ventured, nothing gained.

I decided to make it a spell, and I cast it upon the tabletop, so any work Souris did there would be done pain free. I wouldn't know until the next morning if it worked, but I had high hopes that it might.

My hopes were dashed the next morning, when I woke to the fire burning almost to tinders and Souris grimacing as he tried to slice a poor cut of beef to add to the soup pot for the day.

"I didn't mean to wake you, dear," he apologized immediately, and my heart sunk in my chest. "My hands are especially problematic today."

It didn't work, I thought miserably. If anything, the potion I'd concocted had the opposite effect. Then a clap of thunder crashed outside, announcing the presence of rain I hadn't noticed. If my spell hadn't worked, then the rain could well increase the ache in his hands. I flicked my fingers to the hearth, making the amber ash roar into a blazing flame. The room started to warm instantly.

"Thank you, my dear Salome," Souris said, giving me a small smile. The rain increased, tapping against the stone and the one thick glass window in the kitchens. "The rain, and it is fair chilly. No wonder my hands are so poorly today."

Oui, I thought. *No wonder.*

I flipped back my covers and went to the water bowl to wash the sleepiness from my face.

All my secret endeavors the day before had taken their toll, and sleep fought me and the cold water on my face.

"Here," I told Souris as I wiped my face dry on a torn cloth. "Let me cut the meat and vegetables. You can prepare the broth. I'll wipe the dishes while you take the morning meal up to Adolphe."

Souris eyed the teapot and toast. "More of the same. Not much for me to do as of late. You, my dear, are working far too much. You needed that extra sleep this morning."

I flashed a wide smile at Souris to hide any sign of fatigue. "And now I'm more than refreshed and ready for today. Come, give me the knife and you pour the tea."

Most of my day was spent in the kitchens, relieving Souris of any work with his hands and sulking over my failures in the spell I tried to cast. And the torrential downpour of rain could only be making Souris's hands worse, as it always did when it rained. More than once I had seen him rubbing his hands together, as if he might rub the pain away. Though I kept my eyes downcast, I watched him from under my lowered eyelids whilst he was unaware.

Tonight, I decided. *Tonight, I won't fail.*

I still had several ingredients, and I knew what these were, so I would have to smuggle a book out tonight and try something else, something I was confident would work on him.

Since I wanted to avoid Adolphe's wrath from the spill yesterday, I didn't approach his study until after he'd left, and Souris took a supper plate and another cup of tea up to his room. Then I climbed the stairs, pressed against to the cold stone wall as though I might blend in with it, and snuck into the study.

I did tidy up the room. I tied a kerchief around my wavy locks that stood out in an unruly mess because of the rain and got to work. The book I needed sat on a middle shelf, so I went about the room, setting jars and papers to rights. I made my way over to the shelves and, with a nervous glance at the door, I slipped the book into the bodice of my sagging dress, then rushed out the door to the rear stairs.

The tower was narrow by design, lacking windows or any true amenities. The bottom floor was partially sunken and housed the kitchens and large hearth. Three steps up to the door was the rear exit that led to the woods surrounding the tower, which was hidden away from, well, everything it seemed. Up the stairs was the main level with a small salon-styled hall with the double front doors and Adolphe's study. At the top of the stairs was Adolphe's personal quarters and a small room under the rafters that, until recently, I had called my own.

I tore my gaze away from the stairs leading to the top of the tower. That was my old life. The feel of cool leather pressing against my bosom, the knowledge and power contained in the books, in me, that was my new life. And if Adolphe now despised me or relegated me to the role of servant instead of an adopted daughter, so be it.

As I scrambled down the stairs, clutching the book under my gown, I briefly wondered what would have become of me if Adolphe hadn't taken me in. I knew little of my parents. Both Adolphe and Souris told me they had died in an accident when I was a baby. A cart had overturned, and my mother had used her body to protect me in the crash that neither had survived. Adolphe had found me, taken me in, and he and Souris raised me like I was their own daughter.

One part of me felt guilty about this subterfuge, this going behind Adolphe's back, taking his books and potions, studying without his knowledge. Then I looked over at my pathetic bedding next to the hearth, and the guilt fled. Even Souris had a little room off the kitchen, complete with a cot, a peg for his coat, and a shelf for his candle. He had offered it to me, but I couldn't live with myself if I stole that cot from his old bones. I was young, and my small cubby and pile of blankets near the hearth was adequate for me.

Yet I harbored hate for Adolphe for taking the luxuriousness of my previous life away, mostly for withdrawing his fatherly love. Why had he thought to teach me his magical ways if he didn't want me to learn magic?

Then a thought struck me, as sharp and immediate as lightning hitting a tree. Did he think I couldn't learn? Had it done it to show off, to put me in my place my entire life?

And what would happen if I *did* grow stronger in my abilities? If I superseded him?

I shuddered like icy rain had dripped down my backside. I didn't want to think about that.

For now, I'd be content with my bedding by the hearth.

I slipped the book out of my bodice, set it on my blanket, then shook off my kirtle and hung it on a rough nail above the cubby. I glanced over my shoulder at the stairs, which were dark and silent. Adolphe never came down to the kitchens and never left his room after his supper. The hairs on my arms rose just the same. It must be the storm.

Souris's ramshackle door was closed, in as much as the offset door did close, and no light flickered between the gaps, so he was abed for the night. There was no one but me, with my candle for light, the rain outside to serenade me, and a night of study calling out my siren song.

I moved my toiletries and cape that I had folded inside the cubby to the side and withdrew the leather pouches I'd marked. Sitting cross-legged with the remains of the popping fire at my back, I opened the revered book, taking care not to crease the already worn leather cover, and studied the pages. My finger trailed along the words, searching for something that might help Souris with the ingredients I had on hand.

My hand stopped halfway down the page. There. This one had to work. It had to!

The spell looked simple enough and called for the removal of pain.

It called for cattail, which I had, chickweed, garlic, a bowl of water, and a candle. A tingle flared in my chest as I mixed the ingredients, spoke the healing enchantment, and blew the items into the candle's flame. Then I immediately turned the candle over, extinguishing it in the water, to extinguish Souris's pain.

That was it. I don't know what I expected, but not the dark silence that remained.

Once I was done, I tucked my leather pouches back into my cubby, hiding them behind my belongings again, and set the book on top. My plan was to rise early, slip the book back into the study before Adolphe even woke, and see how Souris's hands fared in the morning with a proper spell to help him.

    I closed my eyes, content with myself. This time, the spell would work, I was sure of it. The magic inside me bloomed as the flowers would bloom after this early spring rain.

    I was coming into my own, blooming like the brilliant roses that surrounded the tower, ready to grow taller, stronger, and more magnificent with each spell I learned.

Chapter Four

It wasn't the crack of thunder that woke me, though it would have if the boot that nudged my ribs hadn't done so a second before. What did Souris want so early in the morning?

"Get up, you thief."

I popped up, holding my blanket to my chest. It wasn't Souris. It was Adolphe.

"Where is it?" he spat out.

The cool leather of his book pressed against my leg and, for a moment, I didn't move. Could I lie? Keep it hidden?

My eyes landed on Souris, who hovered by his own doorway, looking rumpled and defeated in his baggy tunic and stained hose. His hands clutched at his chest. I had a moment to wonder if he realized his hands were clenched in tight fists, an impossible task on rainy days. My spell had worked?

"Where is it?" Adolphe didn't just nudge me; he kicked my mid-section. Not hard, but surprising, and a burst of air exploded from my chest.

I hung my head and reached under the blanket for the book. My hand shook as I lifted it to him.

He snatched the book, then with his other bony hand, he gripped my wrist, wrenching it. I gasped, this time in both surprise and pain. What was he doing?

Souris jumped toward me, but I leveled my gaze at him and shook my head slightly. I'd not have Souris be punished for my actions.

Adolphe forced me to stand by yanking on my arm. He shoved the book in my face, his anger burning off him hotter than the fire that had dwindled to embers in the hearth.

"What have you done? I banned you from magic!"

Courage I didn't know I had filled me, boiling my blood. "You might ban me from magic, but you can't ban magic from me. Why are you afraid of what I can do?"

His face contorted, and I immediately regretted my outburst. His black eyes narrowed to slits, and before I could prepare myself, he lifted me (*did I know he was this strong? He hadn't lifted me since I was a small child!*) and threw me over his bony shoulder.

"I'll show you what happens when you tread where you shouldn't. You will rue the day you disobeyed me." His voice was little more than a growl, and though I strained against him, his arm locked down, holding me in place.

He stormed toward the stairs with me over his right shoulder and his book in his other hand. I tried not to shudder in fear, and as he mounted the steps, I lifted my head and peered through my loose hair at Souris who stood looking forlorn in the kitchens, his fisted hands going unnoticed in the horror unfolding in front of him.

His hands were better. That I knew, and that would keep me while I suffered through whatever Adolphe had in store for me.

I flashed him a sly, reassuring smile and flicked my fingers at the hearth, making the dying embers flare into a brilliant fire. To keep him warm and make sure his hands continued to be pain free. To make sure the fire didn't die out on him.

And to remind Adolphe that I had the power of fire at my fingertips. He might be stronger, but not for long.

I struggled against his iron-like grip, but to no avail. He was mad, beyond mad, irate, and I tried to act brave as my lips quivered and hands shook.

Where was he taking me?

Adolphe huffed as he carried me up the second set of stairs to the top of the tower. His chambers? That didn't make sense. My old room under the rafters? That made even less sense. Once we reached his room, he marched past his door and my old space to the very end of the tower where the roof angled down by the wall. It appeared to be nothing more than stone, but he rested his hand flat against the stone that wept from the rain and the lower part of the wall shifted. I twisted against his shoulder to get a better look.

What is this? A secret room? Was he going to put me in that dark space?

"What are you doing?" I screeched. What *was* he doing?

"Quiet! I'm doing something I should have done months ago."

He lunged forward, and I flipped off his shoulder into the crawlspace, my hair brushing the stone wall. If I were any taller, I would have struck my head and been knocked out, or worse.

My legs stretched out of the tiny room, and I kicked and kicked as he shoved at me.

"Stop! The more you fight, the longer you'll stay! Now pull your legs in or I'll cut them off closing the wall."

I shifted my legs under me and peered up at him. The air was not cool but frigid, and every surface was damp from the weeping stones, but more than that. A leak somewhere? The musty smell of mildew and age overpowered me, and I breathed shallowly with my mouth.

"Why? Why are you doing this?" I wouldn't let him see me cry, but it was so difficult to keep the tears from falling.

Adolphe sneered at me, his black eyes boring into my soul. "I thought you knew your place. I raised you as my own, and you start using magic without my approval? Without my knowledge, even? I am the magician here, not you. Never you. If I want you to use magic, I'll give it to you. Until then, you'll reside here."

"Wait!" I shouted, but he closed the wall so quickly, my words were cut off as blackness fell over me.

I banged on the wall, hoping to find a way to open it. Maybe a panel like Adolphe pressed? A lever? The cold stone cut and abraded my fists until I ran out of energy.

No light, none. My eyes might have been limited, but I still had my hands, and I felt around the inside of the room. A narrow rectangle, most likely built into the back of his quarters. At one point the stone went from weeping to sopping wet – a leak as I'd expected. The rainwater was as cold as the air in the room, a stifling petrichor that in the forest was something from a dream, but here, in this black prison, choked me.

The cool air and dampness quickly seeped through my thin shift – I hadn't even had the time to grab my kirtle or cape. I shivered and brought my knees to my chest, drawing as much of my body inside the linen shift as I could. Then I wrapped my arms around my legs, lay my cheek on my knees, and cried.

And fell asleep. I woke up with my teeth chattering and my face on the cold, damp stone floor. Was there any part of this room that wasn't wet?

Even though I found nothing that might serve as kindling in this crawlspace, I tried to flick my fingers around the room to see if anything caught fire. I didn't care if it was for light or heat, just anything other than the unending cold dark.

Nothing. Nothing in the room could burn.

I don't know how long I slept. Time had no meaning in this room where everything was night. It had been early morning when Adolphe dragged me up here, and while I was hungry, my stomach wasn't growling. Midday at most?

He had threatened to keep me locked up for as long as he desired, until he needed me, but surely, he wouldn't really keep me here for more than a few hours. A full day at most? I have to eat, to drink, and to use a chamber pot.

As if I had drawn Adolphe to me by thinking of him, the door to the crawlspace opened. I shaded my eyes from the light that seemed overly bright after hours in the dark. Adolphe peered down at me inside the crawlspace.

"Salome, are you ready to listen?" His voice held a note of sarcasm, and I wasn't sure if I *wanted* to listen. Everything he said would surely be poison.

"*Oui,*" I said anyway, through chattering teeth. Better off not angering him more.

He wrapped his fur cape around himself and crouched down to look at me directly.

"You've heard me mention the king and his family, correct?"

I nodded. It was an odd question with an obvious answer, as he griped about them all the time. He lamented the king's death and complained about the son, whom Adolphe claimed was a pretentious fool who needed to learn his place. I truly didn't understand Adolphe's distress with the Prince-turned-king.

"The king, the old dead king, we had an agreement. He left me to live in peace, and I offered my services as requested. The village and most of the people in the land were granted autonomy, and I could mingle in the villages easily."

"And the prince-king doesn't let you do that?"

"Look here," Adolphe commanded, slipping his wide sleeve into the recesses of his dark cape and withdrawing a gold-edged looking glass.

I squinted at the mirror, wondering why he was showing me my pale and ragged reflection when the glass fogged up, swirled, and a new image appeared. A translucent appearance of a handsome young man with honey brown hair and a velvet surcoat having an absolute tirade. He stormed about, yelled at others unseen in the glass, and with a wild thrust of his hand, knocked a tall, blue standing vase to the wooden floor, where it shattered to dust. I knew this young man had to be the new king, and I stared in disbelief at this magical glass that displayed his atrocious actions.

"He says he doesn't trust me. His adviser confided in me he's making foolish decisions. I didn't inquire more, but I don't need to. He's a horribly spoiled boy who's become a horribly spoiled king before his time. I would like to have him learn his lesson about what happens to boy-kings when they behave like beasts. If you assist me with this task, you can come out of this room, resume your place and the kitchens, and have my permission to study under me."

He returned the glass to the depths of his robe, and I momentarily wondered how much of his magic he had hidden from me.

Oh, the carrot he dangled. To get out of this crawlspace, I would do pretty much anything. But the offer to resume my magic studies? I silently vowed to make sure whatever task he required was completed to perfection. But there had to be a catch. The man was shrewd. I raised an eyebrow at him.

"Really? You won't punish me for using my magic? You won't feel –"

Adolphe's eyes narrowed. "Feel what?"

Jealous. That was the word that nearly fell from my lips, but that word would only get me locked back up. I searched my mind for a better, more acceptable word. A word that appealed to his vanities.

"Burdened? Teaching me will cause extra work for you."

His face relaxed. My words must have placated him and appealed to his sense of importance. Just as I'd hoped.

"It will be a burden, but one I am willing to accept if you aid me in this. Do we have an agreement? You will do exactly what I ask with the boy-king?"

I nodded. What other choice did I have? He had me in a bind, and he knew it.

"*Oui*," I whispered. "*Oui,* I will help you. Whatever you want."

His thin lips pulled thinner as he grinned. He grabbed her hands.

"*Bon*. Now, let's get you out of here, get you dressed, some food. Warm you up. I trust you can take care of that last one once you are at the hearth?"

If it was an attempt at a joke to smooth this punishment over, it was a pathetic one, but I took it just the same. He was acknowledging my powers, so that had to mean something.

As I crawled out of the dark prison, I had to hope it meant something.

Chapter Five

Souris hid any surprise at my reappearance in the kitchens as he slid a warm mug of cocoa and a bowl of steaming soup to the other side of the table. I slipped my gown and my cape over my head and shoved my frozen toes into my shoes. Before I sat at the table, I flicked my fingers toward the hearth, and the fire roared to life, huge flames that licked the top of the fireplace and gave off waves of heat. Souris's eyes widened at the effect but kept silent. I welcomed the heat after the morning spent in my icy prison.

He watched me as I tore into the warm soup, slurping and swallowing as fast as I could.

"What happened, Salome? Where were you?" he finally asked.

I licked my spoon to delay answering. And there was no way I was going to tell him about my trip to the crawlspace. I wasn't certain his old heart could take that news.

"I took some spilled ingredients from his study, keeping them instead of throwing them away."

"Oh, Salome. Were you trying more magic?"

I shrugged and stirred the limp vegetables in my bowl. "Yes, but only because he all but banished me from his study. I have talent, skill, and I don't want to lose it."

Souris nodded slowly. "I understand how you must feel. So what did he say to you? For punishment?"

Here I had to tread lightly. What had Adolphe said to Souris about the king, the prince, or his dislike for the latter? I couldn't begin to guess.

"He needs assistance with some of his spells and agreed that as long as I did what he asked, I could resume learning under him."

At this, Souris's hands paused in their movements, resting lightly on the table. I noted he was still using them with ease. The spell had lasted. He stilled but didn't raise his eyes to me. "What will he have you do?"

I had started to chew the soft carrots and turnips, but my jaw stopped at the tone in Souris's voice. Not hard or afraid, but cautionary. Wary.

He was worried for me, for what I might have agreed to.

"No, no, he hasn't. But I've completed many spells for him. I don't see why –"

"And this spell? What, he can't complete it himself? Why do you think that is?"

His eyes were yet lowered, as if he couldn't face me as he spoke. His concerns, though, they did give rise to concerns in me. Why couldn't Adolphe do it himself, if he was so great a magician as he believed himself to be?

Echoes of his words earlier – *he doesn't trust you* – and Adolphe's request made sense.

"Because he needs to see the king, the new king, and the boy won't see him, I don't think. He needs a way into the castle now that the old king is gone."

Souris resumed his work at the table, putting scraps in a bin and setting the teacups on their shelf.

"And he believes the king will meet with you? Doesn't that worry you, that he is sending you in to the lion's den while he remains safely behind?"

Curse you, Souris! I thought wildly. Why did he have to shed his mousy behavior now? Until he voiced his concerns, I hadn't really thought about why Adolphe was making this request. And frankly, I hadn't cared. But to hear Souris put it so plainly, maybe there was more to Adolphe's request than I had considered. Given his dreary nature as of late, I couldn't put such schemes past him.

Again, that carrot Adolphe placed before me, of resuming my apprenticeship with him, worked its own magic, and I waved off Souris's concerns.

"It's nothing too dire," I assured him while trying to convince myself. "Anything I do can be easily tracked back to him. I presume he's sending in the young woman to try to placate and charm the boy-king, to help Adolphe gain access to the king as he did with the boy's father."

Souris kept his back turned and didn't respond. He'd said his peace and if I didn't listen, then that was on me.

And truthfully, I didn't *want* to listen. I didn't want to hear his concerns. The enticement of getting back into Adolphe's study, of studying magic and not having to hide it, that pushed all the concerns I might have, or that Souris had, to the back of my mind.

The prospect of magic overshadowed all else.

I had thought the rainstorm was nearing its end – the patter of rain on the roof and stones had nearly disappeared when I went up to Adolphe's study later that day. What met my eyes in his study was chaos.

Every book, it seemed, was stacked, opened, leather spines cracking and breaking under Adolphe's frenzied handling. Jars and pots and bowls littered the table, catching the flickering light of the stone wall scones. Adolphe's hood was pushed back and his graying black hair stood on end, as if his whole body worked in a heightened state. Dried herbs and grasses were spilled on the floor and the shelves while prisms and glasses and gems twisted and turned, making the sconce light dance over the walls and Adolphe in a blend of reds, blues, and greens.

Truly, in all my life, I'd never seen Adolphe or his study in such a state.

I paused at the doorway, trying to take it all in and make sense out of the scene before Adolphe extended a bony hand, waving me inside.

"Close the door! It's nearly complete and then you will have to bring it to him!"

Adolphe's voice rose into a gut-wrenching cackle, and I had the sudden sensation that Souris had been correct in his concerns. An urge inside me begged I leave now and give up whatever crazed endeavor Adolphe had planned.

Then my eyes landed on one of the black leather books on the table, the very one I had filched the night before, and it sang to me, a swan song that mesmerized me into taking a step inside – that single fateful step that sealed my fate with Adolphe.

I knew before I even entered the room that whatever he asked of me, I'd do. I wanted, no needed so badly, to be back in this room, reading those books, my fingers in those pots, and I'd sell my soul to the devil if asked.

And as my gaze landed upon Adolphe in his midnight robes with his hair askew, I wondered if that was exactly what I was doing.

"Here, you will need to take this." He handed over a small velvet satchel that appeared empty, but I knew it held a small mixture, one that was most likely dusty. Adolphe confirmed my suspicions. "When you meet with the king, if he doesn't do what you ask, blow this into his face. It will begin to work immediately."

I palmed the satchel, Adolphe's fevered state rubbing off on me. I was ready to leave for the castle at that very moment.

Before the Cursed Beast

But Adolphe didn't have me leave right away. He gripped my upper arm and led me around to the other side of his worktable.

"The king must complete a task before this spell will work. It's his last chance to show that his behaviors and actions aren't going to lead the kingdom, its people, me, down a dangerous path. To do that, we must play a bit of a trick on him. Can you do that, Salome?"

I stilled, my better sense screaming at me inside my head, yet I nodded, words having escaped me at Adolphe's impassioned entreaty. Tricks weren't significant. Hadn't I been tricking Adolphe when I borrowed his books or stole the contents of his broken jars?

"I must cast a minor spell on you, so that when you reach the castle, you don't look like a pretty young woman, but an old crone. When you get there, you are to ask for shelter for the night. If he takes you in, gives you shelter, then you don't use the potion. You spend the night, come home the next day, and I know my concerns about the boy-king's behaviors were for naught. If he rejects you –"

He paused, waiting to see if I'd respond and understand his intentions. Of course, I did. He was obvious.

"I blow the potion into his face."

Adolphe smiled in a harsh grin and nodded. "*Oui*. But first, you turn back into your real self, so he can see his mistake, understand the error of his ways. You then tell him that for his beastly behavior, he shall be rewarded. Then blow the magic dust into his face. Make sure you do this before any of his guards or advisers discover you. Then leave, cut through the woods, back to this tower."

"But won't the guards chase me? I can't outrun them."

Adolphe's horrible grin widened. "No, no, they won't. You see, the potion affects the entirety of the castle, including those who serve the king. They won't be able to give chase, and none of this can come back on us. And the boy king will learn what he must do if he is to be a leader of the people."

He held up a small crystal cup and swirled the rust-colored liquid it contained. My eyes watched that glimmering, swirling liquid, knowing that with it, my whole life was about to change. I couldn't say yes quick enough.

"*Oui.* I'm ready, Adolphe," I choked out in a raspy whisper.

A sudden crack of thunder made me jump and the russet drink in Adolphe's hand spilled a few drops when he whipped his head toward the single window in the study. His smile curled into a grotesque mask.

His eyes focused on the storm that found new life outside. "Perfect. Who could turn away a forlorn old woman in this weather?" He turned around to face me, thrusting the drink into my hand. "Here, drink. Pull your hooded cape over your head and get ready to leave. He's sulking alone in his own study and will be readily accessible to you."

I glanced at the upside-down mirror on his table. He must have been watching the king to find the perfect time to approach him. How powerful that glass was! I made a mental note for him to show me how to use it once this business was over.

Taking the cup from his hand, I kept my gaze on his thin, hard face as I gulped the drink down. It was sour and acidic, like wine gone bad, and I grimaced as the last drop passed my tongue.

My skin tingled, my scalp, my fingertips. I looked down at my hands – they were no longer olive-toned and smooth. They had paled, nearly white, and deep lines coursed over them like a patchwork quilt and deepened as I watched.

I grabbed the magic glass from his table, and my mouth fell open at my reflection. Only it wasn't my reflection. The open mouth reflected in the glass wasn't smooth and pink, but thin and lined. My golden-hazel eyes lost their glow, fading to a dull yellow, and lines swirled and embedded, making the skin around my eyes sag. My clear forehead was furrowed in thick wrinkles which took over my entire face until I didn't recognize myself at all.

Oh, such power!

"Get your cape and hurry. The potion should last several hours, but I don't want to risk it. Find the boy-king, ask the question, and sprinkle the potion. When you return, you'll go to sleep, wake up your normal young self, and then meet me up here to resume your studies."

Once again, that promise. Seeing how he needed me for this task assured me he wasn't lying. And the task this night truly seemed so minor. If I could help him with this, what else could I help him with?

I stole into the kitchens while Souris was absent and grabbed my cape that I had removed before attending Adolphe in his study. Slipping it over my head, I raced out the kitchen door into the dark downpour.

Chapter Six

Fluttering excitement carried me the entire way to the castle. Adolphe had shown me the shortcut through the woods that would take me to the backside of the castle proper, the secret passage through the stone wall, and the pathway to the door that led to the king's study. That, he had told me, was where the boy king was presently having his tirade.

The rain soaked me to my bones shortly after I left, but seeing the heart of the kingdom rise up between the trees made the miserable weather worth it. How many times had I admired it from afar, wanting to see the castle, its stained glass, and beautiful rooms? And now, here I was, mere steps from the keep.

I approached the door as Adolphe had instructed, but I didn't knock right away. A giant stained-glass window was set into the stone next to the door, and I took a moment to admire the blues, greens, and reds that shimmered in the rain. The raindrops resembled rare gems as they struck the window and cascaded down in jewel-toned rivulets.

A movement on the other side of the window caught my eye, and I leaned closer, resting my palms on the cool glass to peer inside. As Adolphe had promised, the boy king was in his study. I could hear him yelling, muted tones on my side of the window, but not who he was yelling at. Then he grabbed a glass chalice and threw it at the hearth where it exploded in a burst of glass and wine. I jumped back from the outburst and smiled to myself.

Temper temper, I thought as I wrapped my cape tightly around my shoulders and settled the potion satchel in my hand so it was at the ready. Then I positioned myself in front of the door and knocked.

I wasn't sure what to expect from the young king who opened the door, but the handsome man was taller than I'd presumed him to be from the brief time I'd seen him in the mirror. It also hadn't shown his blue eyes, wide and deep set and beautiful. The sharp edge of his jaw, clenched in his fury, showcased every fine line of his face and neck. His surcoat hung open, and the ties of his ruffled shirt were loose, hanging open to expose the honey-brown hair on his chest. He was a thing of beauty.

Too bad his personality didn't match his exterior.

"What do you want?" he spat out as he narrowed those sky-blue eyes.

I fingered the satchel under my cape. It would seem I was going to have to use it.

"Please, sir," I said, making my voice sound wavering and aged. "I got caught in the storm. Might I find shelter with you this eve?"

His handsome face transformed into a hard sneer. Much less handsome now. He dug into a small pocket in his surcoat and withdrew a coin.

"I can give you this, but that's it."

I tried to keep my face from expressing my surprise — the old skin on my face had helped. Why was he offering me coin? My age or the storm? Perhaps Adolphe had been wrong and the boy-king wasn't as miserable as he believed. Adolphe hadn't prepared me for this scenario. He had been insistent about getting into the castle proper, so I pressed forward and asked again.

"I have no place that will take it. On a night like this, surely you can give an old woman shelter?"

"Why would I permit a crone like you into the castle?" He palmed the coin and pulled his hand back. His voice grew even more harsh. He pointed a smooth, slender finger at me. "And how did you get here, to this door? Leave now, before I send the dogs after you."

There it was. I had my answer. This handsome man had the most unhandsome character. Adolphe had been correct about this young man. Spoiled rotten to the core.

"Just one thing," I told him as I readied the powder in my hand.

He leaned his sneer in closer. "What?"

I blinked, and my body flashed so he could glimpse my fresh, youthful face.

"You are a spoiled man and must learn to care for those other than yourself. Until then, your exterior will match your interior," I told him. His wide eyes went wider as he stared at me.

With a simple movement of my hand, I held my palm in front of my lips and blew. The powder took on a life of its own and swirled around his head in a white cloud, untouched by the rain. He recoiled and screeched and waved his hands around his head, trying to sweep away the dust.

I took a step back off the step, ready to run off before the guards came after me, when his hand caught my eye. It was, well, *changing*.

No longer a man's hand, but a larger, clawed hand, thick tufts of brown fur emerging from his shirt cuff.

His screeching became a howl, and I froze where I stood, my eyes riveted on the young man. The hair on his head thickened, growing down his cheeks and jaw, until his entire face was covered. I lifted my hand to my mouth, covering it. When Adolphe had said it would punish his beastly ways, I hadn't imagined it would turn the young king into an *actual* beast.

I couldn't watch any more. I spun wildly and ran, leaving the poor boy-king to his punishment. Hopefully, once the potion wore off, he will have learned the error of his ways and no longer be the spoiled boy-king.

I shuddered to think of what punishment Adolphe might inflict if the man didn't learn his lesson.

When I woke the next morning, my body had resumed its normal age, just as Adolphe promised. Though I'd had a late night running through the wood, I was refreshed, ready to take on anything the day promised, including returning to the study to work under Adolphe. Souris must have noticed my elated state, because he gave me an awkward smile as he slid a cup of tea across the table to me.

He didn't ask me about my night, however. Instead, he placed Adolphe's morning meal on a tray and departed the kitchens without comment. He may not know what I had done last night, but he didn't approve of it, regardless.

I didn't care. I ignored Souris's silent treatment and yanked on my colorless gown. After tying my rain-washed waves of hair away from my face, I made my way upstairs to the study. I'd find something to occupy my time until Adolphe arrived.

The study was a mess from the night before, so I began by cleaning up the books and jars. The magic glass rested on the table, and despite my better judgment, I lifted the glass, hoping it might show the king. Was he still a beast? How long would the spell last? Adolphe had mentioned it would affect his entire household. Would I see any of that in the mirror?

The reflective face of the glass swirled, and the image of the boy-king came into view.

Well, not the king, but the beast he'd become.

He resembled a large dog dressed in fine, ripped clothing. He looked a bit taller, much burlier, but my heart wrenched as I watched him from afar as he sat uncomfortably in a plush chair and wept into his giant clawed hand-paws. I couldn't say why I had this reaction, but something about him touched me deep in my chest.

Oh, the poor king! If this was how he sobbed at his state, then surely he'd be a better man once it wore off! I was certain of it.

"You're up early." A voice broke through my reverie, and I quickly set the mirror back on the table. "Were you looking at the king?"

Adolphe swept past me in his draping black robes and lifted the glass. The king's image was still present, and a thin side smile twitched on Adolphe's lips.

"You were successful, it appears. And he seems to be taken in by his present state. He will learn that if he behaves like a beast, he will become a beast."

He set the glass on one of the shelf walls.

"How long will it last?" I inquired. "Long enough to teach him a lesson, I presume. Several days? A week?"

Adolphe barked out a bitter laugh. "Oh, long enough for certain. He'll die a beast."

Wait, what? I halted where I stood, my hands clenched at my sides. "What do you mean, he'll die a beast?"

Adolphe twisted around, lifting the books from the stack and arranging them on the shelves with his magic glass.

"The final test was last night. I was done with him and his vile behavior. He shall live as a beast, in this form, for the rest of his life."

My stomach dropped to my feet. *What had I done?*

"I didn't know that!" I cried. "You didn't tell me that!"

Adolphe flicked a bored gaze at me. "And what, you wouldn't have done it otherwise?"

"No, I —"

"With how desperately you wanted to resume studying under me? Do you really think you would have done anything differently?"

"Maybe. But shouldn't he have the option to return to his human self if his behavior shows he's changed? If not, what's the point? He'll be a recluse, not a king!"

"It doesn't matter. There's no way to change back. What's done is done."

Though he may have spoken with authority, I didn't miss how Adolphe's eyes flicked to the thick leather book at the edge of the top shelf. I ground my jaw as a flare of distaste burned the back of my throat. Evidently, there *was* a cure to the curse, and it must be in that book. Adolphe might think himself a stoic, unreadable man, but I didn't live with him all my life without learning to read him. Yet I, too, learned something else that day, something that Souris had hinted at, something I should have been more aware of.

I couldn't trust Adolphe at all. He wooed me with words that I longed to hear, then turned those words around on me. I would have to be careful, so careful, under his tutelage. Then, as soon as my magic skills were as refined as I, not Adolphe, could make them, I was going to leave. And I'd take Souris with me, if he were agreeable. In that moment, I vowed to myself. And I swore one more thing.

If I noticed the king started to change his ways, I'd figure out which spell lifted his beast curse and return him to his handsome self.

A man who learned his lesson deserved no less.

Chapter Seven

The hard part would be trying to spy on the beastly boy king to see if he had learned. The glass only showed me a vignette of the king's life, and that was when I could sneak it away without Adolphe looking over my shoulder.

I decided to give the king a week or two, then one night after Souris fell asleep, I planned to sneak out, take the secret pathway back to the castle, and see if I could sneak inside somehow. Watching from the colorful window wouldn't be enough.

When I thought the time was right, I made sure both Adolphe and Souris were asleep, then I wrapped myself in my cape and snuck out the kitchen door.

The night was cool but thankfully dry. Overcast with only a sliver of a moon, so I brought a lantern with me which barely lit myself, let alone any of the trail. Yet I was determined, so I forged ahead. I couldn't let this poor king remain a monster if he was reformed at all. That guilt, having been the one to deliver the potion, weighed on my shoulders and mine alone. Adolphe would have had to find another solution to his problem, one that didn't include me. My determination to study magic had robbed me of my good sense, and now I had to make it right.

I found the castle easily enough, but the exquisite brilliance of the stronghold appeared dimmer somehow. Lifting my cape and skirts, I raced for the side door and peered through the stained-glass window. In shades of blue, green, and red, the beast of a king sunk as best he could into his upholstered chair, the fire in the hearth burning low.

But what really caught my attention was the state of the room. The lush brocade curtains hung in ragged strips from the curtain rods. The painted portraits that had been cut to shreds, jagged reminders of a form no longer his. Junk littered the floor – broken glass and pottery, twisted silverware, tattered clothing.

Was this the result of his actions? Had this king thrown a fit and destroyed his own home? Just how devastating was this curse?

I paused to assess how I might get into the room without his noticing when fortune smiled upon me. A knock at his study door, and the beast king called out in a deep, rumbling voice, so unlike the squeaky one I'd encountered a few weeks ago.

"Who is it?" the king roared, unmoving.

Another voice spoke, lighter, and I couldn't make out the words or see the person, but the person's request must have given the beast enough cause for concern, because the beast rose from his seat.

I blinked my eyes several times. I knew the curse had changed his form yet to see him in his full gigantic animal state! It left me breathless. He didn't just tower over men, he towered over everything. The furniture, the large hearth, all seemed tiny compared to his immense state.

"No, I don't want to attend!" the beast roared again, lumbering toward the door. "How can I be seen like this? Send an emissary and find that strange old woman who cursed me and kill her so I can go back to my normal self. Then I'll attend every event."

His voice broke a bit on his last words, and my heart broke a bit with him.

Poor lad, that's not how it works, I thought miserably. *That's not how any of this works.*

But in my head, I vowed to study the book that Adolphe had glanced at so I might see how this one spell worked. And learn the cure.

I expected the king to slam the door and return to sulking in his chair, but he didn't. Instead, he left, and I found my opportunity.

Even if his study door was locked, which it wasn't, I knew a lock-picking spell I could have used. The door opened easily, and I stepped silently into the disaster of a room.

The floor crunched under my foot, and I glanced down. The shattered remains of a platter, a once beautiful blue and white one. I frowned and watched my step as I closed the door behind me. Then I stared wide-eyed around the study.

Here I was, finally, seeing the beautiful room, the stained glass, the finery – or what was left of it. My heart twisted even harder in my chest. I was finally in the very castle I had admired for so long, and now it was nothing but tatters.

A rustling at the door ripped me from my reverie, and I scrambled behind a side table — a horrible hiding spot, and my lantern was still lit! I quickly opened the lantern window and blew it out. The movement of the beast into the room stopped, and he sniffed the air in huge, slobbering inhales.

"Who's here?" he grumbled in a low voice.

Do I answer? Do I keep quiet? He'd find me eventually, so I erred on the side of confidence.

"It's me," I announced as I rose.

His wide blue eyes narrowed, and he rushed at me, drawing to a sharp halt right in front of the table. My insides shook at his nearness, yet I remained perfectly still as he sniffed around me.

"I know you. You! You're the one who did this to me!"

Then his paw was at my neck, thrusting me against the wall.

I didn't fight back. Rather, I flicked my fingers, making the fire in the hearth roar louder than he, the flames licking the top of the hearth. His grip around my throat loosened as he turned to look at the fire now blazing.

He huffed and turned his ferocious gaze back to me.

"Who are you?"

I tapped his furry wrist with my finger, and surprisingly, he released my neck. I took a moment to rub where he'd gripped my skin. Was I trying to rub away the memory of his touch, or burn it into my memory? What was it about this creature that intrigued me, other than the fact he was a victim of my thoughtless actions? Why was I suddenly so attached to him?

"I am someone who may have made a grave mistake."

His eyes narrowed at me even more, and his snout came close to my cheek, sniffing again. "You were an old woman the last time I saw you. Or I thought you were. Then you were young and cursed me. How are you young again?"

I ran my fingers over my chin as I considered what to tell him. How could I tell him? Truth, as close as I could get, would probably be best.

"I have magic. And I was convinced to use some of that magic on you, mistakenly. My apologies."

The beast stared at me for several heartbeats, his breathing matching my nervous panting, and he stepped away, returning to his chair. He waved a clawed paw at the padded chintz chair, offering me a seat.

Leaving my lantern on the side table, I perched on the edge of the seat. He didn't sit in the chair next to me. His enormous form moved to the hearth, studying the flames that now brilliantly illuminated his study.

"Why? Why did you do this to me?" His voice, which had been so vigorous when I'd first arrived, broke like that of a small, distraught child.

I picked at a loose white thread on the chair's upholstery as I chose my words with care.

"My master, he said your behaviors weren't reflective of the king, that you behaved more like an animal than a king, and he sought to teach you the error of your ways."

His solid frame didn't move as he focused on the ash-coated hearthstones. Then his head dipped a bit, as if he were peering at me from the corner of his eye.

"And you? Did you think me so beastly that you had to change who I was?"

My nail snagged on the chair, and I heaved out a deep breath.

"At first, yes. But I didn't know the curse he set upon you was so dire as this. I truly believed it temporary . . ." My voice drifted off. Looking at him in his wretched form, the words sounded hollow to me, as I was sure they did to him.

His gaze returned to the stones. "Why are you here, then? To mock me? To find joy in the curse you've wrought?"

A knocking came from the door. "I said not now!" he yelled at the poor visitor, and the knocking stopped. He tipped his head at the door. "My entire household has fallen victim to your curse, did you know? Everyone has changed in some obscene manner. What you did punished more than just me."

I bowed my head, my cheeks aflame. Adolphe didn't tell me *that*, either. That anyone other than the king might have been victimized by the curse hadn't occurred to me, and I was shamed by that realization.

"I'm here to see if you have learned your lesson. I might be able to find a way to break the curse –"

At this, the monster whirled around. "Learned my lesson? Who are you to pass judgment on me, one who is your king? I can't be a king like this! I can't leave the castle! I can't visit my subjects or meet with other heads of state!" He rushed at the chair with his fists clenched, leaning into me so the heady scent of his animal musk and wet breath assaulted my senses. "You've not just changed my body! You made me a prisoner in my home! You made my household prisoners! And you want to see if I've learned a lesson?"

He was atop me, and I pushed against the chair, tipping it backward. I sprawled on the ground in a pile of cape and skirts. I hesitated to lift my eyes, afraid I'd find his teeth ready to rip apart my neck.

No teeth. Instead, he roared his outrage at me, his spittle flying into my hair. I scrambled on all fours to the door and raced outside, hoping he didn't give chase.

He didn't. He stopped at the door, clutching the doorway with his giant clawed paws so hard they dug into the stone and howled into the night, a gut-wrenching howl full of sorrow that chased me into the forest.

Once I was in the relative safety of the woods, I slowed my pace and looked over my shoulder. The dim castle had faded into the night as the forest trail darkened. And I'd left my lantern on the side table. Scooping to pick up a fat tree branch from the ground, I wiggled my fingers at the tip, and a small flame leapt to life. Not much light, but enough to let me see the path in front of me.

When I returned to the tower, I stumbled into the kitchens, weary and ready for my bed. My encounter with the beast had sapped me of my energy, and all I wanted to do was sleep.

Chapter Eight

While I worked with Adolphe over the next several weeks, the image of the roaring beast king rose to my mind far more than it should have. Something about the king drew me to him, made my heart wrench and my insides shiver. I didn't know if it was his beastly form I felt responsible for, his rough voice that shook my chest, or the way his blue eyes, so large in their animal form, studied me like the prey I was. Regardless of the reason, a flutter of excitement lit up my chest every time I thought of him.

I longed to see him again.
But I didn't.

Adolphe had used his magic glass several times that first week to watch the beast king's misery, then he'd set the glass on a shelf and forgot about it. He didn't touch the glass again.

And true to his word, he turned his attention to me and my studies, on developing my abilities and skills. He lacked the tender instruction he had shown me before I revealed my fire ability, but he was teaching me, and a beggar couldn't choose from where they received their alms.

After several days of work, however, I noticed that most of the spells and potions were, well, superficial at best. Spells and curses of the level that Adolphe used with the king remained beyond my reach. I needed those spells. I needed that level of skill! How might I change the king back to his human form without it? How was I to leave Adolphe and make my own way with nothing more than love tokens and cleaning spells? I listened like the obedient student, but on the inside, I fumed.

I also noticed that he'd taken to bringing his brown, leather-bound book to his chambers with him, the book he'd glanced at when telling me there was no cure to the king's curse. There was a cure, I was sure of it, and it was in that book – I was also sure of that. But until he left the book in the study, I had no way of finding that cure.

Adolphe had to know I wanted the book, as it was the only book he took with him at night. I'd have to work harder so he dropped his suspicions and left the book behind.

I didn't see Souris much once I started working with Adolphe. Souris left me a simple morning and evening meal, and he was usually abed by the time I returned to the kitchens at night to complete my share of the chores. He was avoiding me, that much was obvious.

And it pained my heart. I longed to tell him I'd realized my mistake in taking Adolphe's bargain and was working to rectify that mistake. Yet, if Souris knew that, might he say something, even accidentally, to Adolphe?

I sighed as I wiped the evening dishes and put them on their shelf. Maybe it was better that I wasn't sharing my life with Souris so much anymore, even though I missed him so much it felt like a kick to the stomach.

When I went into the study the next morning, I arrived with a rag and bucket and a ratty apron over my gray dress. Adolphe had instructed me to scrub his dingy study, and other than sweeping up the spilled jars over a month ago, no one had lifted a finger to clean his workspace. He *could* do it by lifting a finger – I'd seen him wiggle a finger and chant a cleaning spell into place.

Having me clean the study was just another way for him to remind me of my position.

His plan backfired. Cleaning only set me harder on my purpose to become a greater magician and leave his tower, set off on my own, and make my own way. My power and skill were growing – it left like a cannon firing non-stop under my skin, a series of tiny explosions that sent chills and gooseskin over my entire body. Even my hair tingled! And with every spell, every potion, that feeling intensified.

Soon, I promised myself as I scrubbed.

But not too soon. I had to fix the king's curse first, and I needed that blasted book to do it.

I stood on a stool to reach the top shelf, wiping it quickly. Who looked up on the top shelf, anyway? And it was empty, or at least I thought it was. My hand hit something hard, and I grabbed it, unearthing it from a thick layer of dust.

It was a gold-edged glass, a smaller one identical to the larger mirror Adolphe had used to show me the spoiled king. I blew at the dust, my mind in a whirl. Was this also a magic glass? Could it show the same things as its larger counterpart? Did Adolphe even know he had this smaller one?

I wiped the glass clean, and with a furtive glance at the door to make sure Adolphe wasn't approaching, I held the glass in front of me.

"Show me the beast king," I commanded. The glass fogged and swirled just as the larger one had and showed me the king. He sat hunched over on his chair in his study, the hearth cold and gray on this warm summer day. He looked to be speaking to someone, but I couldn't make out anyone else, just his wrecked study items – his books, a clock, a candelabra, and a chipped cup of tea within easy reach. Who was he talking to?

Then I had a flash to the conversation we'd had a few weeks earlier when he cried that he was a prisoner in his own castle. A burst of inspiration flared in my head.

A dangerous idea, but one that I thought might work.

Leaving my rags behind, I rushed down to the kitchens. Souris was still upstairs with Adolphe, so I worked quickly. I wrapped the mirror in the kitchen cloth I'd used on the dishes the night before and tucked it in my cubby.

I couldn't relieve the young king of his beastly state yet, but I could give him a window to the world until I broke the curse.

Adolphe didn't look at me sideways all day, so I must have hid my deception well. I should have felt worse about the mirror, thieving from Adolphe, but I didn't. Rather, I felt empowered, as if I were taking control of my own destiny by righting a wrong. The beast king might not have learned to turn from his spoiled ways yet, but no one deserved to live like that for their entire life, no matter what argument Adolphe gave.

That night, after Souris began snoring gently in his room, I gathered up the glass, wrapped my cape over my gray dress, and slipped out into the night.

Summer had come upon us. No more chilly nights or freezing storms. The nearly full moon and clear, starry sky lit my way down the path.

I half expected the study door to be locked after my last trespass, but it wasn't. I didn't even glance through the rainbow window to see if anyone was in the room. Reckless, maybe, but I was on a quest and wouldn't be denied.

The door opened easily. The study seemed to shift and felt almost alive. The beast rose from his upholstered chair and turned toward me in a slow spin. Instead of launching at me in a rage, his huge blue eyes gazed at me, as though he'd been expecting me. I remained by the door, my back pressed against the stone, the glass clutched in my hand.

"I was wondering if you would return," he said in a low, rumbling voice.

I had no words. I really hadn't thought about how I would give him the glass once I got here, or if he'd even accept it. And he had wondered if I would come back here after our last encounter? Why?

"You ran off so quickly," he continued. "I didn't have the chance to apologize. You were right about my behavior. I can see it now that I'm, well, changed. Even my household staff has commented that I seem to control my temper a bit better."

My lips pulled into a slight smile without my bidding. When he wasn't yelling, he was actually quite the gentleman. Beast form and all.

"Well, silver linings then," I told him.

He gave me what I supposed was intended to be a smile but was more of a toothy snarl.

"Oh, I have something for you," he said, springing lightly on his toes toward me.

I tensed – who wouldn't, having a large, wolfish beast leap at them? He wasn't coming at me, though. He reached next to me to the side table and picked up a lantern.

My lantern that I'd left behind, polished to a glistening shine. The pot of tallow had been freshly refilled, and the wick replaced. My hand automatically reached for the lantern, again, another move I didn't command.

"*Merci,*" I breathed.

"I had it cleaned. It was the least I could do for the way I behaved." He paused, dropping his gaze to his over-sized lower paws that somehow managed to hold up his thick girth. "I wasn't even sure if you were going to return. After last time. I thought to send the lantern to you, but then it occurred to me . . ."

He paused again, as if searching for the right words. He didn't want to suggest that I had broken any rules in seeking him out, and my heart softened toward him again. He hadn't sent the lantern back to the tower because he didn't want me to get in trouble.

"*Oui,* you are correct. I don't exactly have permission to be here. I promised last time that I was going to try to break the curse, and even though you frightened me to my bones, I still made a promise. But it's going to take me longer than I'd hoped. My guardian —"

"*Monsieur* Adolphe Lambert, the tower mage," the beast answered.

I nodded. "*Oui,* he hasn't let the book I need out of his sight. I believe he knows I want to search for the cure and is keeping me from it."

His shoulders sagged, but not as much as I'd thought they would. Had he started to come to terms with his fate? I rather hoped not. I didn't believe we were victims of our fate, rather the arbiters of it.

I set the lantern back down and reached out my hand in a risky move and rested it on his furry arm.

"But I won't give up. Again, I promise."

He looked down at my hand. "You're touching me. You aren't afraid of me?"

I pressed my lips together and looked him in the eyes. "I came back, didn't I?"

The beast king straightened, pressed his other arm across his waist, and bowed regally for an animal.

"I don't believe we've been formally introduced," he said. "I am his Highness, Prince Faustin de Villepin, now king of Lyonnaise Provence."

My side smile returned to my face. I followed his lead with a sweeping curtsy. "And I am Salome Martin, apprentice magician of the tower in the wood."

Then he surprised me by taking my hand off his arm and lifting it to his wolfish lips, presumably kissing it.

"The pleasure is all mine," he said as he straightened. Then he gave me that wolfish grin again. "Now that the pleasantries are out of the way, why have you returned? Not many beautiful women attend the castle as of late."

Oh, did my cheeks heat in a fiery blush! When had I ever been called beautiful before? Never. No compliment ever crossed Adolphe's lips. And Souris's compliments were focused on my duties or abilities, not my appearance. My tongue lost the ability to speak.

"Or did you return just to retrieve your lantern?" the beast asked, filling my awkward inability to form words.

I shook my head hard, gathering my wits. My hood fell back, and the beast's eyes widened briefly as his gaze coursed over my lush chestnut locks, then his attention refocused on my face.

"Oh, *non*, not for that. But I do thank you for your care of it. *Non*, I have something for you. A gift, if you will, as you wait for me to fulfill my promise."

His furry, furrowed brow was comical, and I bit the inside of my lip so I didn't laugh aloud at the poor king.

"A gift? You don't owe me a gift."

At this, I did let the giggle inside me bubble out. "That's the point of a gift. It's a gift, not a payment. It's not owed."

"Your laugh is enchanting," he blurted out. My whole body inflamed this time, not just my cheeks. I dropped my gaze to the glass in my hands.

"Oh, well, *merci*." I held up the gold-edged glass for him. "This is for you."

Faustin didn't take it right away. He stared at it as though I was handing him a snake.

"A mirror?" he said in an odd tone. "Do you seek to prolong my agony by showing me my horrid state?"

His engaging banter had disappeared, replaced by sorrow.

"Oh, *non*!" I placed my hand on his arm again and tugged him gently to his chair. "Here. Sit. Now, take the glass in your, uh, hand."

He begrudgingly did as I bid, settling in an awkward posture. I slipped the handle of the glass into his paw. The beast king averted his gaze, as if his own reflection pained him. I imagined it did.

"Look into the glass for a moment." I kept my voice light, encouraging. He did as I asked. "Now this is no regular glass, it's magic. It will show you whatever you desire to see. Anything. Name something outside these walls you want to view in the glass."

He grumbled, disbelieving, then spoke. "Show me the village."

The glass fogged up and swirled for him just as it had done for me. His eyes blazed as his reflection faded and the image of the sleepy nighttime village came into his view.

"Is there something specific you want to see in the village? Or someone?"

The beast shifted in his seat. "Show me the tavern."

The glass swirled again and showed the only place still awake in the town – a raucous tavern where a handsome, black-haired man held court with a mug of ale and drank heartily with his friends.

The beast's agitated features softened as he watched the camaraderie of the tavern's guests.

"Last time, you said you were a prisoner," I explained, resting my hand on his shoulder and leaning in on him. "That may be true, for a time. But this can show you the world outside the castle until you can leave the grounds yourself."

To my surprise, he lifted an immense paw and patted my hand. "This, this is such a generous gift." Then he shifted his frame around to look at me side long. "But, this glass. It belongs to your guardian, am I correct? Surely he will miss such a divine piece of magic."

I shook my head. "*Non*. He has another one. A larger one. This was covered in dust on a high shelf. I daresay he forgot he even had it. He won't miss it at all."

The beast kept his paw on my hand, light but dense, as if he was holding back every possible violent emotion with that one hand.

"*Merci*," he said breathlessly. "I've never received such a gift for no reason other than to be given a gift. My parents, *oui*, they gave me gifts, because I was their son. But none other than that." He looked back at the men cheering in the glass. "Nothing like this."

He continued to watch the men's antics, then shot up straight in his chair.

"My dear Salome! It grows late! I fear I have kept you far too long."

He was right. And I still had a fair walk back to the tower, yet I waved his concerns away. I was truly enjoying myself with him. Other than Souris, who'd I known forever, Faustin was the first friend I ever had.

"It's not too late." I hedged around the truth. "And the walk is short and will be easier now that I have my lantern returned."

I stood up and stepped to the door. He followed close behind me. When I spun to say goodbye, he grasped both of my hands in his. My heart stopped beating, I was sure of it. He kissed one hand, then the other.

"*Merci*, again. Do you need an escort home? I can find someone . . ."

"*Non*," I told him in a shaky whisper. "There's a hidden path that cuts right to my tower. And you are most welcome."

I withdrew one of my hands and wrestled with the handle. The door opened. I pulled back on my other hand, grabbed the handle of the lantern, and slipped out into the night, which was now somehow more splendid and invigorating than it had been when I'd arrived.

When I reached the castle gate, I glanced back over my shoulder. The beast stood at the doorway, watching me as I rushed off into the night.

I don't know what I was feeling, but something in his voice, how he treated me, the light touch of his heavy paws, struck deep in my chest and bloomed like a peony in spring. Although he might feel alone, I'd make sure he never truly was. He didn't believe anyone would want him or love him as he was, but after today, I knew a truth in my heart.

"I would love you," I whispered into the night air as I walked dreamily through the wood, heard by none but the trees and the stars twinkling above.

Despite the enormity of what I'd just done and the lateness of the hour, I smiled to myself the entire way home.

Chapter Nine

The next morning, I rose to the sounds of Souris bustling in the kitchens. He didn't comment on the bags under my eyes or the lateness of the hour. Instead, with downcast eyes, he slid my toast and hot chocolate across the table. He may have been curious as to what I'd been doing, what I had done to hone my magic, but he didn't ask. Did he not want to know, or did he fear what my answer might be?

I didn't care for this distance between us, but I understood it.

I offered no response or hint at where my magic journey was taking me. And I certainly didn't mention anything about visiting the boy king. Not really a boy king – no, the king I'd spoken to the previous night was a man through and through. Faustin may be an enormous grotesque beast, but a man lived and breathed under that fur and those fangs. I saw it in his cerulean eyes when he gazed at me, when he peered eagerly into the mirror.

Rather than risking a conversation with Souris, I silently ate my buttery toast while he prepared Adolphe's tray. At least Adolphe was yet abed. Souris might not inquire as to my tardiness, but Adolphe wouldn't pass up the opportunity to interrogate me over it.

I hustled through my morning routine and was tugging my shoes over my heels as I raced up the steps to the study. Giving it a full assessment, I made certain every jar, every book, and Adolphe's own larger magical glass were all in place. We had been working on animal spells over the past several days, so I took the initiative to set up the jars, bowls, pestles and books that Adolphe might need for the day's potions and charms.

In truth, I had memorized most of the potions in the book he'd been using with me – they were fairly basic, but now I had access to the ingredients to bring those spells and potions to life. And oh! The tingling sensation those skills brought me, from the crown of my head to my fingertips . . . it was almost as powerful as the fluttering in my body when the beast king entertained me. A monstrous beast, *oui*, but his appearance didn't detract from his engaging eyes, the rich tenor of his voice, his powerful presence.

"Salome! Do you have everything ready for today?"

Adolphe's sickly squeaky voice interrupted my thoughts, and without thinking, I glanced at the top of the shelf before looking at him. Had he noticed my gaze where the small magic glass had laid hidden and dusty until I pilfered it?

He didn't seem to – his black gaze focused on the table, readied for his attention.

"*Oui*, Adolphe. I brought out the *Animalis* spell book. I presumed we were still using it?"

Oh, but that I had a spell to hide my desires! I felt like they were painted clear on my face, and Adolphe was the one person who might read those desires.

"Hrmph," he muttered under his breath as he stalked into the study, his black cape dragging on the stone floor behind him. He set the brown leather book on a high shelf. "We will use the *Animalis* book today, but by now you should have those mastered. They are simplistic spells, after all. If we finish early, we will crack open the *Volo* book later this afternoon."

He gave me an eerie, toothy grin, which I'm sure he assumed was intended to reassure me, but it sent a chilling shiver down my spine instead. It was as if he had seen straight into my mind and could read my thoughts.

I moved to stand next to him at the table, then stopped hard. From under my hooded lids, I snuck a glance at him. Who was to say he couldn't read my mind? That he had that ability, and that could be the reason he predicted so much about me, manipulated me so easily.

As of late, my blind faith in my guardian had started to wear away, as the sea crashed against the stones, wearing them down until they were smooth and glossy.

Was that what he'd done to me? Did he have the power to read my thoughts and use the knowledge he gained to wear me down, make me pliable?

And what of the glass? If he had such a power, then he'd know I stole away, met with the beast king, and gave him the mage's magic window to the world. I shuddered inadvertently as this swell of realization pounded in my head.

"Are you well?" Adolphe asked, not looking at me. "You seem suddenly pale, Salome."

I shook my head quickly and stepped to his side. He used to seem too tall, so commanding, and though I wasn't an overly tall woman, I had caught up to his shoulder. And he'd aged, started to bow. He didn't resemble the imposing spell caster of old.

I should be able to withstand him, assure him naught was amiss.

I certainly found myself no longer impressed by him and his position. If I dropped my girlish blinders, what I saw before me was nothing more than an aging man in a threadbare cape.

Even if he did manage to read my mind about the mirror, I wasn't worried. I was growing stronger as he was getting weaker. How much longer could he wield power over me? Not much longer, surely.

If my training kept up, I might even be able to restore the beast king sooner than I'd expected.

Turning my face upward to Adolphe, I gave him the most cloying smile I could muster.

"*Non*, Adolphe. Excited. Let's get to work so we can move onto the *Volo* text."

As promised, he brought the *Volo* book down from its place on the shelf. I'd managed to thieve it a few times before, but never had the chance to truly peruse those thin, delicate pages. Now I had all the time in the world, and a master spell caster to show me the nuances of each potion.

And access to the necessary ingredients. In less than a week, I had mastered most of that book as well.

Now, I barely had to flick my finger to start a fire, and I could do it with the barest of kindling. I was able to use my spells to keep Souris's hands free from pain most of the time. I don't know if he noticed it, but I did. Controlling temper, changing fortunes, moving clouds to bring storms and sunlight, creating cleanliness from decay and vice versa, all at my disposal. It was enough to make my head swell.

We were more than halfway through the text, and I was waiting for him to bring down the brown leather-bound book, the one he'd flicked his eyes at the day after I'd cursed Faustin. Yet days passed, we neared the end of the *Volo* book, and nothing.

Patience, I told myself, which was easy for me to say. I wasn't trapped in the body of a beast.

That night as I straightened the study, my eyes flicked to the narrow window. The woods were shadowy just beyond.

Easy for me to have patience, but what of Faustin? He had to live in that body and would need reassurance. He should be aware that I was working on the solution to his curse, but I needed more time. Heavens forbid if I were to try to break the curse and failed, only to keep him a beast forever.

My chest clenched at that possibility.

For a moment, I wondered if Faustin was watching me through the glass. I hadn't considered that he might do such a thing, but as I was the one who cursed him, then vowed to break the curse, I imagined he studied me to see if I was going to keep my promise.

Poor Faustin. I had to let him know I was working on it.

At that moment, I decided to sneak out again. To visit Faustin.

I told myself that it was to assure him I hadn't forgotten my vow.

But my heart, well, my heart knew the truth.

I wanted to see Faustin, to be gazed upon by those gold eyes that tilted the earth under my feet. To be the sole focus of his powerful presence. To see my friend, whom I'd come to love as more than a friend.

Adolphe's door slammed shut – Souris had delivered his evening meal and was going to find his own bed for the evening.

I bided my time until Souris was asleep in his bed, then once again, I slipped out into the night and sought the beast king.

Faustin threw the door open as I stepped into the yard. I raced inside his study, my cape swirling around my skirts as he drew me in for a suffocating hug. My senses raced at his embrace.

"How did you know I was coming?" I asked.

If a beast could blush, I imagine that was what Faustin did. His entrancing gaze danced from me to the small glass table next to his chair. The mirror rested face down, within easy reach of the armrest.

"My apologies, dear Salome. I know you gave me the glass to watch the world around me, but after you left, nothing in the world seemed quite as interesting."

My heart stopped in my chest. Fully stopped, and I couldn't breathe. What happened to the air in the room? Why was it so thick? Why couldn't I draw it in?

Then he lifted my hand and kissed it so gently, I saw the image of the man under the beastly fur.

I couldn't move, not until he swept his hand at the plush chair and spoke.

"Will you have a seat? I'll have tea brought in."

I nodded. I had no words – they were as lost as my breath. I sat.

Again, that odd movement in the study caught the corner of my eye as I watched Faustin call for his servant at the door. When Faustin spoke to him, he had to crouch low, which was odd. Hadn't the butler been a tall, slender man? I thought I'd seem him the night of the curse, but perhaps I was mistaken.

And when I pulled my gaze from the powerful beast near the door and glanced around the room, that odd sense of movement stopped.

It must be the effect the beast was having on me. Why was I feeling like this?

Faustin held up one clawed finger from the door, and a few moments later, he held an exquisite silver tray between his giant paws as delicately as he could manage. I jumped up to help him and set it on the table next to the side door.

"You're not angry?" he asked as he poured tea into each flowered porcelain cup. Yellow irises decorated his cup while mine was painted with dark pink peonies. "At watching you in the mirror, I mean?"

"*Non*," I answered as I cleared my throat. My words, and my breathing, had returned, if only just. His nearness, the breadth of his chest and shoulders – for some reason I couldn't draw my gaze away. "I understand why you did it. I'm sure you're watching that I am keeping my promise to somehow break this curse."

His large paw lifted the dainty cup, such a contrast in size it seemed almost comical, and he handed it to me. I took it without thinking. "Sugar? Milk?"

"*Oui,* please, both."

My lips played at a smile as his thick, furry fingers used the silver spoon to scoop a heaping pile of white crystals into my cup, followed by pouring the creamy milk from a bluebell painted creamer.

I took a deep sip when he was done, hoping it would calm my nerves. The sugary, creamy delight tasted somehow better than any tea I'd had in my life. When I lifted my eyes to his face, he was studying me, his brilliantly blue eyes capturing me and not letting go.

"*Non,*" he answered in a low, harsh tone. "I watched you because you are the sole beautiful person in my life. I couldn't take my eyes from you as you left. I tried not to see you in the mirror. I didn't want to invade your privacy, but I was powerless. Not a day passed that I didn't ask the glass to show you."

Did I blush? Oh, that is too light a word for the blazing heat the surged from my belly to my head. My hand shook as I tried to take another sip.

"I saw you in your, uh, place where you do your spells. The man in black, he's your teacher?"

"*Oui,*" I answered, finding it easier to talk about Adolphe than myself. "I'm studying as much as I can as fast as I can. I think the way to remove your curse is in one of the older books, but he won't break that open until he thinks I'm ready."

A low, growling chuckle emerged from the beast's chest. "Oh, have no doubt. He knows you're ready."

"What?" Tea sloshed as I jumped in my seat. I grabbed my cup with both hands lest I dropped it. "What do you mean?"

Faustin shrugged and set his cup down. It tipped and should have spilled, but it oddly caught itself and righted. How had it not spilled?

"I mean," he said, redirecting my thoughts, "that you don't see it, because your attentions are on your spells or bowls or books, but *he* knows. I think you're much more powerful than he lets you believe. The look on his face when you lifted your finger at the window and the skies grew dark . . ."

The beast king didn't know what had transpired in the study that day. That had been a weather spell, and the clouds had shifted at my command. Adolphe made it seem like a simple enough task that a child could do it.

"A weather spell," I whispered. "What did you see?"

I set my own cup down and rested my hand on Faustin's huge, furred arm. He leaned into my touch, as if he needed it, having missed being touched for so long.

"His face. Pure shock is the best way I can explain it. Have you ever seen him move the clouds?"

No, I hadn't. In truth, I hadn't seen him do much at all. In fact, as of late, I'd done all the spells, mixed the potions, said the words.

Made the curses.

I searched the beast's face to see if he was telling the truth. His shining fangs, his long muzzle, the thick fur might hide the truth, but his eyes, the most endearing and expressive eyes, they searched my face as I searched his.

His eyes were more readable than the mirror I'd gifted him, and the blue majesty of his gaze told me the truth that I would receive from nowhere else.

Not from Adolphe who didn't want my skills to supersede his.

Not from Souris who feared me and barely spoke to me anymore.

Not myself, who had lived in the shadows of a treacherous man my whole life.

Without realizing it, Faustin and I had pulled together as my mind raged, until my face was mere inches from his furry, fanged muzzle.

His head bowed, the rough fur on his cheek brushing my face, and my heart stopped as the light sensation.

"You should go," he growled. "I live for the moments you might visit me. But if you stay longer, I may not be able to let you leave." Faustin's voice was a hard whisper in my ear.

I didn't move, not right away. With a slow movement, I pressed my hand against his other cheek, holding his furry face against mine for a long moment.

Then, in a rush, I backed away and turned toward the door.

"I'll go, Faustin. But I'll come back. I don't fear you the way you think I should. If anything, you should fear me."

He kept his gaze lowered, unmoving from where I'd left him.

"I could never fear you," he said, his rumbling words vibrating in my chest.

I bolted from the door and ran for the woods.

Chapter Ten

I ran until I was breathless for another reason, not because of his nearness, but because my body couldn't run any farther. Even then, I still felt the heat, the power of his presence, and the rumbling vibration of his voice deep in my chest.

What had happened? He was a boy king I'd cursed! Why was I visiting him, befriending him, touching him . . .?

Falling for him.

I slapped my hand to my chest, trying to control my pounding heart and lungs. I leaned against the trunk of a thick alder tree for support.

This night! Too many things happened this night. My emotions roiled over the beast's closeness, his observation of my skill, my realization that I'd have to find out if I could break the beast's curse now.

No more waiting. I couldn't torture him with the curse any longer.

I hiccupped and dropped my hands to the rough tree bark.

But if he wasn't a beast, would he still want to see me? Would he see me as beautiful and engaging if he didn't have to hide, if he had a world of ladies to choose from?

I didn't know. And if I was honest with myself, I didn't care.

He was a friend, more than a friend.

Though it was dangerous, I knew I'd return to his study as often as possible.

And break that hideous curse.

Despite my better judgment, I couldn't stay away from the king. Something about him was so different. He wasn't an older guardian like Souris. He wasn't a hardened adviser like Adolphe.

He was a young man, not much older than myself, in a horrible position that I was responsible for putting him in. And he was a friend, the first person I have ever called a friend.

How was I supposed to stay away from him?

And if something inside me melted every time his fair eyes and furry face glanced at me? Well, that was something I was going to have to deal with.

After all, I wasn't about to fall in love with a beast, was I? Even if I did, what good would it do me? The fact I'd changed him into a monster would always sit between us like a thorny rose bush, prickling away at us and drawing blood until we were drained dry.

No matter how much I cared about him, or how much I loved him, I had to set that aside and focus on my spells.

At least, that's what I told myself over and over, as if my brain might convince my heart.

But the mantra was useless. I wanted him. I wanted that giant beast in all his animalistic traits. I longed to have him look at me with his ferocious intensity, hold my hand in his clawed paw, speak to me as if he really wanted to hear what I had to say, and take me away from the cold, dark tower that had become my prison as of late.

I wanted to bask in the light of his stained-glass mirror during the day and stand by his side, not hide in the shadows.

A dreamer I might be, yet I was a pragmatic one. I convinced myself that visiting him was a kindness, locked in his castle as he was. That I could visit him and keep my friendship and heart separate.

So I went back. Again and again, I returned, until one night when I did have news for him, such news that might bring the light back into his dreary life.

After Souris had snuffed out his bedside candle, I burst out of the kitchen door, my cape flapping behind me, and raced into the welcome arms of the night.

The trail through the woods was becoming worn from my travels, and familiar that I no longer needed a lamp or lantern, even on the darkest of nights. Bushes no longer whipped at my legs or caught my cape, having been broken or beaten back by my nightly excursions to the castle. On one trip, I marveled that I had lived so close to the castle, so close to this young man with whom I'd found great affinity, yet had never traveled there until that fateful, stormy night.

The backside of the keep rose in a darkened outline against the summer night sky, and I raced past the gate and through the study door without looking into the window.

That had been my mistake.

I had known that Faustin was hiding something mysterious about the castle from me — the fact I'd never seen a single other person there, not a butler, not a maid, not a servant, should have made me question it more. Yet, he deserved his privacy and secrets. Who was I to bully him into revealing anything to me after what I'd done? If he wanted to keep his life beyond the study private, then I respected that.

But what I saw when I lurched through the door was nothing that I might have expected. Or imagined.

It was a dog, a larger black and white papillon. The animal stood on his hind legs and held a tray out to Faustin, who froze wide-eyed when I exploded through the door.

I snapped to a stop, pulling up short just inside the doorway.

Whatever secrets I'd believed Faustin to be hiding, a servant dog was not it.

We three stood in the study for several heartbeats, staring at one another, until the papillon bowed his head and dropped to all fours. He exited the room with his head and tail held high, a proud beast. I couldn't tear my eyes from the animal until he walked past the door and kicked it shut with his hind leg.

My mouth hung open, and once the door slammed shut, I turned my gaping jaw to Faustin, who had dropped his face into his gigantic paw, the picture of embarrassed misery.

I blinked several times and finally found my words. "Not only you?" I whispered, my hands clutching at my cape.

Faustin nodded into his paw.

"I thought the curse was for you. Adolphe stated you were spoiled, a wild animal, so he wanted to teach you a lesson. I had no idea . . ."

He raised his face and set his intense gaze upon me. His face was tight, hard, an angry beast ready to pounce on its prey.

"You had no idea that your master transformed not only me, no matter how guilty I was, but the innocents in my stronghold, too?"

My hand crept to my mouth, covering it as if it might cover the horrific realization of my deeds. I hadn't merely cursed one man — my curse had harmed many other innocent people whose only crime was loyally serving their king.

Faustin might have been the beast, but I — *I* was the monster.

Non, I said to myself. *Adolphe is the monster. How could he do this to a group of innocent people?*

"Is everyone in the castle like this?"

Faustin's strong, tall shoulders slumped. He must have believed me when I said I had no knowledge of the depth of the curse.

"*Non*. Some are. A few servants. They're dogs. Some became rats —"

At this, a squeaky, scurrying sound came from behind his chair. I leaned to peer over the back of the seat. A pair of large brown rats sat up on their hind legs and wiggled their noses at me.

With my eyebrows high on my head, I pointed behind the chair. Faustin nodded.

"Remember when you commented that the study felt alive somehow? Most likely, Barie and Gerard were running from your arrival. They have nooks and hidey-holes everywhere in here."

The scurrying sound shifted and the rats, Barie and Gerard I presumed, scuttled to the base of the hearth and disappeared into a small hole in the stones. I squeaked louder than the rats at their rapid departure.

"The rest, they became like statues. Some carved into the stone, some into the beams, some into the silverware, residing in whatever room they were in when you arrived that fateful night."

He didn't say it, how kind he was. But I needed to say it out loud, to take accountability for my actions against him and his servants.

"When I came here and cursed you all," I finished for him.

Faustin shook his head wildly and stepped toward me. He reached out his hands and lightly pried mine from my cape.

"*Non!* Your master made you do this, and you did not understand the depth of the curse. That blame cannot fall on you."

He paused and tilted his head, eyeing me nearly sideways.

"What?" My tone was more clipped than I'd intended. I was angry at Adolphe for using me this way, and angry at what my own actions had wrought.

"You didn't know what you were doing with that curse, yet you had enough power to change an entire king's household. In that moment, your master should have had an idea of your power. Does your master understand the strength of your abilities? How strong is he, then? He can't be that strong if he had to send you to do his work."

I had no response for that. The suggestion that I might somehow be stronger or more powerful than Adolphe was one that I eventually hoped might come true, but not now. I had only started —

"Oh, that reminds me! That is why I'm here!" I exclaimed.

His paws clenched my hands so tightly, my bones ground together in my hand.

"You have found the spell to break this curse?"

My face fell. Oh, why had I sounded so excited when he mentioned my skills? I dropped my gaze and shook my head.

"*Non*. Not quite yet, but this day, Adolphe drew the final spell book from the shelf. It is ancient and thick, and I don't know how long it will take me to master the needed spell, but I have that book at my disposal. It's the same book he looked at when I asked him about a way to break the curse. He claimed no spell like that existed, yet his gaze drifted to this book. I promise you, Faustin, if the solution is there, I'll find it and make it for you!"

He tipped his head again. "And you don't fear what Adolphe will do when you achieve this? He will know what you want the spell for, what you intend to do."

I opened my mouth to answer, then snapped my lips shut. I hated to admit that I hadn't quite thought my plan out that far. My intentions were to break the curse. What happened after that . . . Well, I hadn't considered *that* at all.

"He will probably put me out, maybe try to reinstate the curse. I truly didn't consider that. I only thought . . ."

Faustin pulled me closer to him as my words drifted off. His musky heat enveloped me, comforting me.

"Maybe you didn't think about it because you didn't need to. He sent you to curse me and my household. Maybe, underneath everything, you know that when he does find out, you can handle anything he might throw at you."

I shook my head in his furry chest. "The only thing he'll throw is me into that wet crawlspace again," I muttered.

"If he does, could you get out?"

I didn't answer right away. Faustin was walking me through something, trying to help me see something beyond the veil.

"*Oui.* I have a lock-picking spell. I could easily get out."

Faustin was silent for a moment. The only sound was his heartbeat pounding under his thick chest.

"Why is he showing you all this? Why is he giving you the ability to be stronger than he? That doesn't make sense. He has to know the breadth of your abilities by now."

My mind swirled as I clung to Faustin, his words and their logic wracking in my brain.

Why *was* Adolphe doing this? Why would he give me the keys to the tower, in a sense, if I could use them against him?

Because he didn't expect me to use them against him.

He believed he could keep controlling me.

But how? Not through a spell — I would have caught on to that.

Then what or who —

I stopped.

Souris.

If I threatened Adolphe's power and position, he had Souris under his thumb. And Souris was no magician, no sorcerer, no wizard. He was an older man, a servant, and at the mercy of Adolphe.

All the blood raced from my head as I swooned on my feet as the world went dark.

If Faustin hadn't been holding me upright, I would have crumpled to the ground in a faint.

But he held tight, and I managed to keep my feet.

That wasn't enough for Faustin. With an effortless movement of his arms, he swept me up off the floor, clutching me protectively against his chest, and brought me to his overstuffed chair. He settled me in it, my legs thrown over one arm and my back angled against the other. He cupped my head for a moment, then moved easily to the door and called for his servant, the papillon dog, I supposed, and requested tea.

He returned to my side, and with an awkward shifting of his legs, knelt beside me. With his giant form, he curved over me, as if guarding me from Adolphe, or the knowledge I had of him.

"What is it, Salome? Does he have something on you, something to control your powers?"

Adolphe might try to threaten Faustin, but Faustin was a king with power of his own. The fact Adolphe had sent me to curse him told me that Adolphe's power or control over the boy-king was limited.

He might try to threaten me, but what could Adolphe do that he hadn't already? And I would counter anything he tried. Further, I had little concern about what he might attempt with me — I had already suffered so much that I didn't really care if he tried to hurt me.

I lifted my teary gaze to Faustin. "Souris," I whispered raggedly, trying to hold back my shocked tears.

"The man servant? The one who cared for you?" His own voice was low, a growl but not a fearsome one. A warning growl.

"*Oui.* He has nothing but his work for Adolphe. No family, and his bones are starting to ache, so it's difficult for him to work. I've cast a spell on him to rid him of his pain. But if I'm not there to cast it upon him regularly . . . Or if Adolphe puts him out . . ." I sobbed as fiery tears of understanding burned my eyes.

"Or worse," Faustin grumbled, and once again, I covered my mouth with my hand.

How much could my mind handle this night? This was too much. The realizations of my actions, or what will happen with my actions, made my head swim like I'd swoon again.

A rough, scraping knock came at the door. The dog servant with our tea. I yet struggled to believe what my bleary eyes saw before me.

Faustin took the silver filigree tray with a gentle paw and brought it to me. He set it on the hearth in front of the low-burning fire, the silver reflecting the flames and making them dance along the stones. I closed my eyes, lest the image pain my mind more than it already was.

"Here." Faustin handed me a teacup, one with pink roses this time, and I accepted it with a shaky hand. "Did you truly not have a plan for what you would do once you undid Adolphe's curse?"

I nodded and sipped my tea but didn't taste it. I barely swallowed. "What do you think I should do?"

Faustin shrugged one shoulder as he slurped his own tea. Droplets clung to the fur around his snout when he lowered his cup.

"I had thought to ask you to stay here. I can easily hide you from the man. But I hadn't considered anyone else might be at risk." Faustin lowered his head. "If you cannot undo the curse because of this, I understand," he said in the most dejected tone I'd ever heard. And my heart throbbed painfully in my chest to match the pain in my head. Here he was, giving up his chance to become human again to save me.

Oh, Adolphe, you were so wrong about this young man, I hissed to myself. Even if he needed to learn a lesson, only a good man, a truly good man with a large heart, scarified himself for another.

And Faustin was a good man. I was certain of it.

An idea struck my head so hard it pounded like a hammer on an anvil. *My poor head*. I sat up tall in the chair and set the cup on the small table next to the chair.

"Souris could stay here!" I grabbed both of his paws, unsettling his tea that spilled onto our hands. "Souris is a servant! He can leave the tower right away, and you could hide him from Adolphe and his threats!"

The beast didn't move. He stared at me as though I had grown another head.

"Did you hear me, Faustin? I can still complete the spell and undo this curse! If you keep Souris here, then he can't be used against me to keep me under Adolphe's control!"

Faustin didn't respond. His eyes bored into mine as he weighed my scheme.

"If you think Adolphe can't harm him here —" he started, hope filling his voice again.

"*Oui!* I don't think he can! Don't you see? It's why he sent me to curse you! He's not strong enough to do it himself. If he can't come here to curse you when you were yet a green boy, then he certainly won't try when you are back in human form, a great man and powerful king. Or he'll fail if he does try."

I didn't know if my eagerness at this sudden plan startled him, but he stiffened as he stared at me. Had I overstepped? All I wanted was to undo this terrible curse and not harm anyone else as I did it. Was I asking for too much?

"You think I'm a great man?" he asked, his voice tight.

I squinted at him, then lifted one of my hands to caress his furry cheek. "I don't think you are a great man, Faustin. I *know* it."

He panted as I spoke, his burly chest heaving, and the air in the study grew thick as we gazed upon each other.

"You can't know that," he countered.

I raised my other hand and cupped his other cheek, pressing my face close to his nose. "I do know that."

Before the Cursed Beast

"How? How can you know that? You haven't seen me do anything as a king!" His disbelief made him sound like a little boy. I smiled.

"Nothing you did as king showed me. The night I came back here to admit my crime against you, did you throw me out or threaten to hurt me? *Non!* You listened to me, forgave me, and welcomed me into your home. That, my sweet, is the measure of a great man and powerful king. One who has the absolute, ruthless power, but exercises care and consideration. *That* is what a great man does."

He dropped his muzzle and closed his eyes, absorbing my words. It appeared that both of us had shocking realizations this night.

Then he nodded between my palms and lifted his gaze.

"I would do anything to help you, to save you, even if it takes you forever to undo the curse. If all it does is get you away from this terrible master who trains you, I would do it for you. Send Souris here when you can. He, and you, are always welcome in my home. Make it your home."

My home. After a lifetime in a cold tower, sleeping in corners and on cold stone floors, not a place I might call home in any sense of the word, to be offered a kingdom as a sanctuary . . . Such a generous gift.

And in that moment, I knew. I might have tried to convince myself otherwise, lie to my heart, but my heart knew the truth.

I was in love with this beast.

And from how he gazed at me from where he knelt on the rug, I believed the beast loved me as well.

Chapter Eleven

I fairly danced as I walked home, my mind spinning as I recalled our conversation and the realizations we'd had. I also made plans. To search that book, get that spell, gather Souris and our belongings, head to the castle, and change the beast and his household back to normal.

It seemed a simple enough plan.

I just needed to finish reading that book.

The next morning, I was up early — even Souris still dozed in his tiny closet — and crept up to the study to start reading the book. Adolphe might not like that I was reading it without him, but he was the one who'd brought it down from its place of reverence on the top shelf and gingerly brushed the thin layer of dust from its ancient brown cover. Sewn in a darker brown thread was the image of a sun nestling into a quarter moon. Odd writing was stitched underneath that image. I hadn't touched it then, but this morning I traced that image and those words with my fingertip.

"The *Book of the 1st House*," Adolphe had intoned with a touch of pride. His chest swelled as he presented the book and set it on the table. "This is the book that contains the most powerful of spells, unlike any you've seen before."

My mind had immediately conjured up an image of the beast. "I'm certain. Will I learn all the spells in the book?"

Adolphe had pressed his hand against the cover. "Most of them," he'd said.

But I hadn't fully believed him, and I didn't believe him now in the fresh light of day. Not after my harrowing conversation of discovery I'd had with Faustin.

I had closed the door halfway and kept flicking my eyes to the hall. I also listened to every sound in the house as I waited for Souris to rise and bring Adolphe his morning meal. Though Adolphe had shown me the book the day before, pointing out some of the first spells and potions, I had the sense his anger would have no bounds if he found me reading it without him.

The key unlocking Faustin's curse was in this book, after all.

As my fingers threaded the pages, flipping through spells that would protect one from the evil eye, get a woman pregnant, and recover a dying relative, I had a moment to wonder *why* he was showing me the book if the manner of breaking the curse was in it. It didn't make sense to me. Did he plan on skipping that spell, thinking I wouldn't notice? Was he going to rip that page out of the book, or had he already?

It seemed a ridiculous way to keep me from learning how to undo the curse.

Footsteps echoed on the stairs, the slow gait of Souris bringing Adolphe's meal to him. I silently shut the book and moved to the far side of the room, checking jars and noting which ones were low. When Adolphe appeared, it would seem as if nothing was amiss.

Adolphe arrived at the study door shortly after Souris had shuffled his way back downstairs. I sat at the table with a parchment in front of me, noting the items and ingredients that were low. I looked up when the door swung open, but Adolphe didn't enter right away. Rather, he lingered in the doorway, his black eyes studious and the side of his mouth curled into something that resembled a grin.

A gut-clenching, nefarious grin. My breathing raced at that grin.

"You are up and ready to start. That's a good thing," he said as he crept into the room, the length of his cape dragging behind him. He almost looked happy?

No, that was the wrong word. Nothing made Adolphe happy.

Smug. That was the word. As if he'd finished an arduous task and the completion pleased him.

I nodded at him, then looked back at my writing. "I'm making a list of necessaries, for the next time you go to the apothecary's."

"Mmm," he mumbled as he moved to the table, right next to the book. I watched him from the corner of my eye.

"Did you read more of the book? You must be excited to learn the more difficult, powerful spells."

His tone. Why did he sound like that? I flicked my gaze from him back to the book, and then to Adolphe again. He stood with his hand

resting flat on the text, still nearly grinning.
Grinning.

Something wasn't right. I sat up and looked at him straight on.

"Yes, a bit. To see what was coming up and check our ingredients, as I said."

"Only a bit?"

He was taunting me. The hairs on my arms rose up, and a chill coursed over my spine. He was taunting me for a reason, and I didn't know the reason. I kept my face as bland as milk, pretending his mocking wasn't getting me worked up.

But it was. I didn't want to answer him.

"Yes," I replied flatly, "a bit."

His long, bony finger slid between the pages, nearly two thirds of the way into the book, as if marking the page.

"Are you sure you didn't read this page?"

He flung the book open and flipped a few pages over. When he found what he was looking for, he slammed his fingertip onto the page. "This spell here?"

That sickening grin was back on his face, and I paused in my writing.

A chilling sensation crept up my backside. I leaned over the table to peer at the spell he pointed at. The dreaded curse. The inked script was old, ornate, and bled into the aged paper.

Taming Behavior with Dire Consequences.

I blinked several times. He was showing me the exact curse he had me put on the young king.

But why? What was he doing? Why show me when he had to know that I would use it to cancel out the curse?

He spun the book at me, so I could read the full spell text. "Why don't you read it?"

My face was stoic as I stared at him for a few seconds, then I grasped the book and slid it close to me. I hung my head over the page as I read the words. The impossible words that brought me back to that night when I had done the worst thing in my life.

The curse was familiar enough. I followed the lines with my finger to make sure I didn't miss anything. What did he want me to read that I didn't already know? I flicked my gaze up at him and his smug grin. He tapped the book.

"Be sure to read all the way to the bottom of the page."

I bowed my head and skipped down to the end of the curse. The bottom line, in bold lettering, told of how to undo the curse. Or rather, how *not* to. I froze in my seat as my eyes read and reread the words that had blurred together in my disbelief. My throat closed as I lifted my face to stare at him, unable to hide the stricken horror that surely covered my face.

Adolphe stared at me, his black eyes wide and jubilant at what I'd just read. "I know you saw me glance at the book the day you cast the spell. And I knew you would get to this book soon enough, if not read ahead, to find the spell and undo it. But I wasn't worried. Why would I be?"

His nefarious grin widened, his yellow teeth long and full in his mouth as he uttered a bone-chilling, barking laugh.

"All this work, your studying, and I see how strong you've become, how confident in your skills, but all for nothing, wasn't it?"

My hands shook as my fingers curled around the book's edges. My insides melted into a sludge that curdled in my stomach. I launched myself off the stool and raced downstairs, my hand over my mouth, and burst out the kitchen door. Vomit exploded from my mouth into the grass right outside the kitchens. I heaved and heaved until there was nothing left inside me. Nothing at all.

I had made a promise to the beast I thought I could keep — it was the reason he had befriended me, the reason he grew to care about me. The reason he promised Souris and I could come live with him, despite what he said about undoing the curse.

It was all because I would break that curse one day.

And Adolphe, in all his sick power, had shown me that no matter what I did, or how skillful a magician I became, or how much I loved Faustin, I had no power to break this curse.

In fact, *I* was the only person who couldn't.

Souris found me bent over the dirt by the kitchen door and rested a comforting hand on my back.

"Salome? Are you unwell?"

He may not have spoken to me in weeks after my first encounter with the beast king, but the concern in his voice told me he hadn't misplaced his love for me. I stood up and wiped my face with my sleeve. My poor kirtle, splashed with mud and vomit. I'd have to do a round of laundry today on top of my other chores.

Yet, I welcomed the extra work. Anything to keep me out of the study and away from Adolphe and his games. Far away. And give me time to come to terms with what I had learned today.

"*Oui,* Souris," I croaked. "My morning meal must not have agreed with me. Maybe the bacon I ate had turned. I'm feeling much better now. Should we go inside?"

He plastered a fake smile on his face that didn't reach his eyes. He was unconvinced by my story and worried about me.

I didn't blame him. I worried for me. For him. For the beast king.

I pressed my hand to my forehead as Souris led me into the kitchens. What was I going to do? What was I going to tell Faustin?

Souris set a cup of water in front of me. "Here. Rinse your mouth. Then find your other dress and let's wash that one. I have water already boiling at the hearth. We can use that to launder your kirtle. Will Adolphe miss you in the study today?"

He knew Adolphe wouldn't miss me — I realized that from how he asked the question. I shook my head. "*Non.* We have been so busy, and he has commanded that I catch up on my chores. I've been leaving too much for you as of late."

Souris stepped to the hearth to check the water with a ladle, his hands moving with confident strength. Not a grimace or a groan from Souris.

I had to do something. I couldn't let Souris suffer from his aches and pains, take the abilities of his hands away. I had to make sure that he ended up safe and protected from Adolphe, no matter what I ended up doing.

"*Oui,* the water is quite warm. Go behind the curtain and change. I'll retrieve the soap and the other pot."

Souris and I spent the day together, laundering my dress, scrubbing the kitchen tables, washing dishes. I remained focused on my quiet contemplation, trying to figure out my next move, as Souris chatted lightly about everything and nothing. He didn't appear bothered that he had only a fraction of my attention, and I was grateful to him for that.

I wanted to have a plan before I met with Faustin again, a solid strategy of what we would do next to break the curse. But I had nothing. Not a single idea.

I dreaded telling Faustin. I dreaded what he would say or do when I told him I had to break my promise. Because I had no other solutions at my disposal, no other spells that could break the curse and return him to his human state.

I had failed him. And he was going to hate me for it. My heart ached, a deep, agitated ache, and I wanted to avoid going to the castle, avoid telling him.

Yet I feared the longer I waited, the worse it would be.

I sighed. Best to get it over with.

Chapter Twelve

On any other day, I'd race as fast as my legs could carry me to reach the boy king's castle, but not today. This night, I dragged my toes in the dirt and stopped with every thorn that caught my threadbare cape. The night wind rose, making my hair swirl around my head, and I shuddered but not from any chill in the air.

I shuddered because I had grown to care for Faustin, even to say I loved him, and now I had to deliver the most devastating news, let him know I couldn't keep my promise to him. Surely I'd break his heart, and in doing so, my own.

Part of me longed to believe he would understand – that he might hear my story and Adolphe's role in it, as the master crafter of menace and heartache, and he would understand that this wasn't my fault. In my deepest imagination, he took me into his furry, heady embrace and lowered his face to mine. I didn't care if he was a beast. He was beautiful to me, inside and out.

But saying he didn't care if it took be forever and actually knowing that to be the case were two different things. No matter what he had told me, breaking the curse *was* important to him, important to his ability to be a true king to his province. And I had robbed him of that.

I might love him, but any feelings he had for me were surely going to transform into hatred the moment I told him the truth. That was what the other part of me believed. No matter how much I loved him, or how much he might care for me, our feelings for each other and the ability to remain friends, let alone anything more, hinged on my ability to return him to his human form.

I paused at a sagging alder tree and pressed my forehead against the rough bark. It was nothing more than added delay, stopping at the tree, and I knew it.

He was going to hate me.

I think that knowledge wrapped around my brain more than any other.

He was going to despise me, and I'd be fortunate to make it out of his study with my skin unbruised and my bones unbroken.

I'd seen the state of his study before he put it to rights, how he had destroyed it when he was first changed into a beast. He had ripped curtains, tapestries, upholstery, and canvases to pieces. Even the once-beautiful portrait of him as a younger man that had hung above the mantle was nothing more than shreds in a broken frame.

Shelves, tables, decor, candles, all had been smashed, broken, destroyed. The hearth itself, the stone monolith that dominated the large wall of the study hadn't escaped unscathed – I had noted more than one set of claw marks and the chipped stone. In his anger, had he tried to peel the stones apart?

An impossible task, I was sure, but he'd still let his anger rage so violently, even hardened stone succumbed to his fury.

What chance would my tender skin and delicate bones have?

I shivered under my cape again and glanced back at the way I'd come. It would be so easy to go back to the tower, slip into my bedding, and pretend that fateful day last spring hadn't happened. Forget the boy king existed and return to the dismal banality of my life.

My head swiveled in the other direction, where the stately edge of one roof line peeked from behind the trees.

No matter how much my fear shouted at me to return to the relative safety of my tower, my heart screamed louder – to see Faustin and risk that he might, in some small, tremulous corner of his heart, forgive me.

That possibility encouraged me to keep going, to turn toward the roof line and not back down the beaten trail. That one, slender grasp of hope, that thin chance that Faustin might, *just might,* understand that I, too, was a victim in all this, and not destroy me.

My fingers flicked of their own accord – and my heart leapt in my throat. He might *try* to destroy me. But it would only be *try*. Because we both knew what havoc I might wreak with a movement of my fingers and a phrase from my lips.

However, unlike Faustin, I knew something he didn't.

I'd never use my magic against him, never again.

Faustin wasn't the only one who learned his lesson that stormy spring night.

The wind kicked up, and I wrapped myself in my cape and emerged from the wood at the rear of the keep.

Unlike my previous visits, I didn't race in. I didn't run to his study, to his company, to his arms, ready to spend an evening of meaningful conversation with him. Instead, I paused at the gate and stared at the giant, multi-chromatic window that was shadowed and gray on this night. It seemed to reflect the darkness of my consciousness and soul.

The study door creaked open, and Faustin's gigantic frame filled the doorway.

"Salome? Why do you linger by the gate? Come in. Anton has prepared a fine drink of frothy lemon water for us."

He reached out a clawed paw, and on any other day, I would have reached for it unhaltingly, his paw as comfortable and familiar to me as my own hand. I didn't see a beastly paw, I saw an extension of the boy king, the beast I'd grown to love.

I stayed by the gate.

"Salome?" His voice carried across the small yard, still deep and resonating, but with a hint of caution.

He knew. I wasn't the unflappable sort. Every emotion showed on my face, no matter how much I practiced with Adolphe. That evil magician saw my every thought, and not because he read my mind. I'd come to realize that he wasn't powerful enough to do that with me. No, it was because my face betrayed my every thought.

No wonder Adolphe had been able to use my own skills against me and set me on this path.

I inhaled a deep breath and took slow, tiny steps as I approached the door. His face, normally wide and open, was screwed up, his furry eyebrows low on his brow. He took my hand in his, untangling my fingers from my cape to do so.

"Salome, please. Is something wrong? What has you so fretful this night?" Then a rough growl emanated from his chest, vibrating me to my bones. A growl of unrelenting fury. "Has he hurt you in some way? Are you injured?"

Oui, I said to myself, *only not in the way you think.*

His enormous paw cupped my head, making my hood fall against my back and exposing my rich chestnut waves to his view. His thick, clawed fingers threaded my hair, rubbing my head, and I nuzzled the pads on the palm of his paw.

Then I snapped my head up and moved toward the hearth that burned low, more for light than heat. One other short, fat candle burned on the table. The rest of the study was enshrouded in shadows as Faustin liked it, so he might not see his beastly self reflected or in the full light.

Oh, poor Faustin! To be forever stuck in those shadows! No man, least of all a king, should suffer such a fate. Not for the first time, the bitter bite of acrid hatred surged in my throat at Adolphe and his machinations.

"*Non*, Faustin, not injured. Not like that."

He grasped my hand and pressed it between both of his, as if he wanted to keep touching me, as if he were afraid to let me go. I relished his touch for as long as his touch lingered, knowing it might be for the last time. I took a few shallow breaths before speaking, my breathing finding the same pace as the broken-face clock tucked into a dark corner. I dropped my gaze. I couldn't look at him as I spoke the words.

"Adolphe showed me the book," I whispered, barely louder than the ticking clock. "Showed me the curse."

Faustin, who had been gently bent over my hand with concern, straightened, stiff and tall, dwarfing the room. I hadn't realized until that moment how often he bowed himself to appear less fearsome. In his full breadth and height, he was a frightening beast indeed.

"The book?" his voice rumbled. "My curse?"

He still held my hand, but he was so stiff that he was squeezing it, nearly to the point of pain. Yet I didn't pull away. I deserved that pain.

"*Oui*. Your curse."

I flicked my gaze up at him. His eyes were no longer an engaging blue – they were hard, as sharp as his claws that bit into the skin on my wrist.

"You aren't happy. You aren't ready to break the curse. What is it? Why won't you do it?"

I couldn't stand it anymore, and a silent tear slipped down my cheek, staining my skin in salt and self-hatred.

"Is it because you think I won't want to be around you anymore?" he continued. "That I won't keep my promise to keep you and your friend safe? That I won't want to be around you anymore once I'm out in the public, the king I should be? If so, that's not true. I'm not that person, Salome." He paused, bowing his head so it moved closer to mine. And I was already having a hard time breathing! "At least, not anymore. I vow to you, Salome, you will be as welcome in my castle as you are now."

Could he have said anything worse?

No, because now I had to admit I couldn't keep my promise, and why. What manner of person quashed one's vow by breaking their own? That bitter taste of bile burned my throat again.

"I know," I whispered in a wavering tone. "I know you'll keep your vow. That's who you are. Who you've become."

"Then what?" his voice lowered, still rumbling but less harsh. It caught my heart in a web and twisted it.

"Faustin, I read the curse –"

"And how to break it?"

I nodded and dropped my gaze again. My throat was so thick, every word I wanted to speak got stuck in it.

"Then what? Do I need to do something? Do you? Do you need some items or special ingredients? I can buy . . ."

Eagerness replaced the low caution in his voice, and again, my heart wrenched. He yanked on my hand, drawing me closer to him and forcing me to look up at his face. His handsome, beastly face.

"Tell me!"

"I can't!" The words burst out of me before I could stop them.

He stilled again. "You can't tell me what you need? Or you can't break the curse?"

His voice was so low and gravelly, it was difficult to make out the words. I didn't want to make out the words. And I didn't want to answer.

But he deserved more. I lowered my head; I couldn't bear to look him in the eye anymore.

"I can't break the curse."

No sound, no noise but that stupid clock. Faustin didn't make a sound, but the feel of his hot breath on my face told me he was still bent low, still close to me. Then a ragged sound tinged his breathing, growing louder, becoming growling. I steeled myself, cringing under my cape.

Then his growling became a roar – a powerful, bone chilling roar unlike any sound ever cried out before. It bellowed up from his belly, through his vibrating chest, and out his gaping, fang-edged mouth. The windows rattled to match my bones, and the silver vibrated on the table. My fingers tingled, ready to twitch at the slightest need, but I inhaled deeply to keep my fingers in check.

The vow I'd made to myself to not use my magic against him was one I *would* keep.

His roaring grew louder, and he finally released my hand. He spun toward the hearth in a flurry of fur and fury. He roared and scratched at the stone, scraping and clawing until the pads of his paws bled.

I didn't move. I didn't try to hide behind the chair or cover myself with my cape. To what end? I didn't want to hide. I wanted him to see how sorry, how pathetically sorry I was.

His rage burnt itself out for the moment and he spun again, this time on me. He pressed his face against me, his sharp teeth nearly nipping at my cheek. My insides quivered against my will.

"Why can't you? You told me you could do it! You vowed to me that you would find the way to break it and do so! Now you come here and tell me you can't! Why not? Why won't you do it?"

I didn't cringe or cower back from his teeth, his steamy breath, his accusing words. I stiffened my back to remain right where I was.

"It's not that I won't, Faustin," I told him in an unsteady voice. "Adolphe may not be as powerful as I am, but he's much more worldly and much more conniving. He tricked me. When I confronted him the day after I made the curse, he knew if he flicked his eyes at the book that I'd believe the solution lay in that book."

"So what? It doesn't? It is somewhere else?" His hot spittle flew against my cheek. I closed my eyes but didn't flinch away.

"*Non*, it's in the book. But I can't do it."

"Why, Salome? I thought you — I thought we — Why?" He was flustered, tripping over his words, and I had the sense that my feelings for him were not one sided. If he had loved me as I loved him, then this was the ultimate betrayal.

Taking a chance, I lifted my left hand and rested it on his burly, panting chest. The pain of what I was about to say was significant, and I wanted to touch him as long as I might. For he'd throw me out and I'd never touch him again once I finished speaking.

"To break the curse, you need to have someone fall in love with the beast, to see beneath the fur and fangs and love the man underneath."

His puffing breath halted as he took in my words.

"But, I thought –" he started, then tried again. "I know that we never said anything, that neither you nor I said the words, but I thought you did . . . I mean, I love . . ." Again, he stumbled over his words, and I understood why.

"I do, Faustin," I choked out. Now the tears fell freely, and I didn't stop them. I clung to his chest and stared up at him. "I love you, Faustin, in a way I hadn't known possible!"

"Then, why isn't the curse broken? Do you not love me enough? Because I would do anything for you, Salome, I'd give my own life for you, I love you so much! Don't you love me enough? Is it because I look like this that you can't love me that much?"

I began sobbing, unable to control it anymore. How could I convince him of how much I loved him? Words weren't enough.

"I do," I sobbed, pulling back from him until only my fingertips touched. "I love you more than my own life. I'd give myself for you, but that's not it. Not at all."

"Then what?" he breathed.

I stared at him, keeping him at an arm's length away. My insides shook, but my voice was forceful when I finally spoke.

"The very person who casts the curse is the sole person who *cannot* undo it. Adolphe planned it that way. He knew I'd undo the curse in a moment he'd cast it. But having *me* cast it means *I* can't undo it, no matter what I do, no matter how much I love you. I'm the one person who *can't* undo the curse."

Chapter Thirteen

His face fell, and he stepped backward. He turned to show me his back, leaning against the scarred hearthstones.

"Faustin –"

"Leave, Salome," he said in a despairing voice. "Just leave."

I opened my mouth to try again, but to what end? And if I said something that angered him? Then what? I'd seen what he'd done to the stones, and though I didn't really believe he'd hurt me, sometimes our emotions can be too much, overwhelm us, and make us act in ways we'd regret later. Worse, he might say something that injured me more than anything his claws might attempt.

Better to not walk the line of that regret.

I gave the inconsolable beast one last look before I threw my hood over my head and slipped past the study door to the bleak, dark outside. The heavy shroud of despair that hung over both the beast and me seemed to permeate the air and hang over the entire castle and spread before me as I made my way to the woods.

The farther I walked, the more my anger and my sheer hatred for Adolphe grew. Like a fire in my belly, consuming the kindling of my frustrations with Faustin, it was fed by my desire for a manner of control, of autonomy, in my own life.

Would a time ever come where Adolphe didn't have a sick finger in every part of my life?

My fingers twitched as I walked, and the grass by my feet lit on fire – a flame that matched the fire inside. As the flame jumped to another patch of grass, I had an awareness of what I'd done. What if the entire forest caught fire because of one thoughtless movement I made in anger?

I moved to the side to step on it, but when I lifted my hand, the fire extinguished on its own. Nothing but a wisp of smoke in the darkness and the arid scent of scorched earth.

I stared at the wisps I could barely see.

Why had the flame gone out?

My heart pounded in my chest and my skin prickled as an idea rose in my head. A painful, immense idea that couldn't be true. Couldn't *possibly* be true.

I flicked my fingers again, igniting another patch of grass. It flamed a dim orange, dancing as it searched for another piece of grass to feed on. With a burst of inspiration, I wiggled my fingers, and the flame stretched, reaching almost, to jump to another blade of grass. Then I wiggled my forefinger at the next patch of grass, and the flame reached again.

Non. It wasn't possible.

I crouched close to those flames licking at the air, and with my forefinger, I waved it to the left, then the right, and the flames followed my fingertip.

It was me. *I* controlled that flame.

I swept my fingers around into a fist, and the flame immediately dropped, extinguishing.

I stared at my hand for a moment, then reached down and touched the crispy, burnt earth. The dirt and scorched grass were warm and smelled of burnt flora, but the fire was gone.

That flame had emerged, grown, and died at the mercy of my fingers. I didn't merely light fire.

I controlled its every movement.

Swinging around, I stretched my hand forward and snapped. Both sides of the pathway lit up as brilliant as the noonday sun. Then, when I swept my hand into a fist, the flames were gone, as if they never existed.

What had happened? What had made my skill grow in such a stark and sudden way?

I lifted my face to the cloudy skies.

What else could I do?

Without a word, I raised my hand above my head and thought of the moon coming out, the stars bright against the black sky, and the clouds shifted, parting like milky curtains enough to let the slice of a moon and a few scattered stars appear.

At this, I froze. I had hoped the spell for clear skies I'd recently learned would work, but I hadn't expected it to. Not without potions and charms and speaking the words.

But it was all under my control with only a flick of my hand. I shuddered.

No wonder Adolphe tried to keep me under his thumb.

He *had* to.

Otherwise, I'd easily overpower him. I had never seen him do anything like this. All his spells were contained within his grim study, limited by his ingredients and the words in a book.

Contained.
That word.

It defined my entire life.

Until I had cursed the beast.

That curse — it had done more than change Faustin's life; it had changed mine.

And my skills had grown significantly stronger since I'd known him. Had knowing the beast, my friendship with him, my love for him, created a power inside me? One that Adolphe couldn't compete with because he had no heart, no love, for anyone but himself?

I wiggled my fingers at myself, and a spark jumped from one finger to the next.

If I didn't have to dance around Adolphe, I could do so much more. I could protect Souris, keep his hands free of aches. I could search every book, every spell, until I found the one to break Faustin's curse.

I would be in control.

And in that split second, I made a decision.

I was done being held under the weak oppression of Adolphe's thumb. That was all going to change tonight.

I burst into the kitchens louder than I'd intended. I went right to my bedding and my cubby, throwing my belongings into a sack. I had no plan, but I'd leave tonight. I'd find a place to stay, even a hut in the woods, until I figured out what to do, where to go . . .

"Salome? Where have you been? Adolphe asked for you earlier."

I whipped around. Souris peeked around his closet door, his gnarled hand gripping the edge. He was pale, paler than I had recalled seeing him before. Was he worried? Afraid? In pain?

"Souris, I'm fine."

"What are you doing? I had to lie to Adolphe, telling him you were getting eggs from the chicken coop, but I think he knew I was lying. He had that look. Where were you? Why are you packing?"

My whole body sagged as I dropped my gaze to my feet. As much as I wanted to strike out on my own, the memory of my conversation with Faustin about Souris haunted me. I couldn't leave Souris here. Adolphe's anger would have no bounds, and all that fury would fall upon the meek and subjugated Souris.

I lifted my gaze to him and opened my mouth to ask, but the sight of his balding head shining through his thin white hair and those gnarled hands made me snap it shut. Souris *had* to come with me, or I had to keep him safe, and he couldn't live in the woods with me. He was an old man, and service in the tower was all he knew. Robbing him of that lifestyle would be cruel. I had few options.

"Salome? What's going on?"

"If I had to leave, Souris, would you go with me?"

He opened the door wider, his incandescent light shadowing his face from me. "What do you mean? I would do anything for you, Salome. I've told you, you are like a daughter to me. But where are you going?"

I leveled my gaze at him. "If you had to leave Adolphe, you would?"

Souris barked out a hard laugh. "I don't stay here for him, my dear. I stay for you. I might have left years ago, but to leave a small girl in his rough hands? Only an evil man would do such a thing." So much love for the undeserving me! Souris left the doorway and walked up to me, an arm's distance away. "Salome, please, tell me what's going on. I'm worried about you. I've been worried about you for a while. And with you sneaking out . . ."

My breathing caught in my chest. "You knew?"

His face softened with a gentle half-smile. "Of course. But you needed your privacy, and I figured you'd tell me where you were going, eventually. And you've been so happy as of late, I guessed you were meeting a young man. Does that have anything to do with this? Has he asked you to go away with him?"

Oh, mon chou! Quite the opposite.

"*Non*, nothing like that," I lied. I glanced at my belongings hanging out of my bag. "And *non*, I have nowhere to go. What I do know is we need to leave. We need to get away from Adolphe. I can't stay here with him anymore."

Souris reached for me, resting his hand on my shoulder. It was a light touch, and he didn't grip me. Were his hands paining him? His watery gray-blue eyes studied me, questioning me. I took a deep breath.

"This is why I need to get away from him. Watch."

I slipped my hands from my cape. I flicked my fingers at the hearth, which instantly leapt to flaming life.

He glanced at the fire, and faced me again, barely registering the flames.

"Salome, you've had that ability –"

"*Non*, Souris. Watch."

He tilted his head to look at the fire. I spread my palms wide, and the fire bloomed hard, the flames licking the top of the fireplace. Souris cowered toward me at the blast of heat.

"Salome –" he gasped.

I waved my hand down, and the fire disappeared completely. Souris's hand clutched my shoulder, and if he had any pain in his fingers, it was forgotten at the sight of my control of the fire.

"What –" he breathed.

"There's more."

I called upon everything I had learned over the past weeks. Narrowing my eyes and wiggling my fingers, I made the broom and dustpan prance across the stone floor. For the plates drying on the counter, I wiggled my fingers, and the plates flew like birds to their shelves, clacking lightly as they stacked themselves. The window opened, and I swept my arms toward myself, mumbling the words I had committed to memory under my breath for added effect, and a breeze, at once cool and refreshing, blew in through the window. Souris's night shift and thin hair flapped in that breeze. He uttered an odd sound, gripping me harder.

I slammed my hand downward. The window slammed and the broom and dustpan fell to the floor. Everything stopped.

Poor Souris was panting, his face pale and his eyes bulging wide.

"Souris?" I asked. Had I shocked him to death?

"Salome," he breathed again. "What is all this? How did you –?"

"I've been studying, learning, and I've become so powerful . . . But I can't stay here with him anymore. We have to leave."

Souris's eyes scanned the kitchens, as if still seeing the dishes and broom dance.

"Where would we go?" he asked absently.

That was the question. I might live off that land, but Souris could not do that. And my chance to live with the king, have the castle as sanctuary, was lost when I told Faustin about the curse. Where would we go?

"Yes, where would you go?" a harsh voice called from the stairwell.

Chapter Fourteen

Souris and I spun around and latched our arms to one another. Adolphe stood on the bottom step, partly covered by shadows.

What was he doing in the kitchen? He never came down to the lowest level of the tower. Whether he saw it as beneath him, or he didn't desire Souris's or my company — both options were equally possible — he didn't descend into the tower depths.

Yet here he was, standing tall and confident, staring at us from the black depths of his eyes.

"Sir, we were cleaning. . ." Souris's voice wavered as he spoke.

"Silence!" Adolphe shrieked, lifting a bony hand toward Souris, who snapped his jaw shut. Adolphe turned his menacing gaze to me. "Where are you planning to go, Salome?"

His tone was light as he spoke to me, sending a shiver down my spine, and my mouth went dry. I gripped Souris's thin arm.

"Away," I squeaked. I hated how my voice sounded, as though I feared him. I *did* fear him, but I didn't want him to know that.

"Away where?" he asked, again lightly. His fingers trailed along the stone wall as he descended the last step into the kitchens. Souris shook under my grasp.

I swallowed, trying to wet my dry mouth. "Away from you."

"Mmm," he muttered. He sounded almost like he was indulging a young child. Taunting me like I was a little girl, someone trapped under his roof and at his mercy.

A flare of anger, much like the flame I'd snapped to life in the wood, lit inside me. He had treated me like that my whole life, keeping me imprisoned, making my life not my own. And here he was, doing it again with little more than his tone of voice.

Non! The flame inside me burned higher, scorching my throat, and my skin was fevered.

"And how do you think to do that?" He remained by the steps, long and daunting in his black cape and nonchalant pretense.

He had to be planning something large, something grim to keep me sequestered here as his prisoner for life.

The palm of my hand was hot, burning, the flame ready to burst into my hand.

I narrowed my gaze at him. He was going to learn that I was no longer under his control. He'd learn what it meant for me to have full independence from him and his sinister ways.

But Souris stood right next to me. One wrong flick of my wrist, one wrong word spoken by Adolphe, and Souris might never recover. I had to get him out of the way.

I turned my face into Souris's night shift, as if I were cowering from Adolphe, and spoke in a tremulous whisper I hoped Souris heard.

"Offer a tea to Adolphe and move to the table. When I lift my hands, run to your closet and lock the door."

Souris stiffened under my feverish hands. He'd heard me.

Would he do it? Or try to convince me to stop?

And if he did as I asked, could I defeat the old, wizened magician and win our freedom? Or would Souris suffer for my pride?

We were going to find out.

"Master Lambert," Souris spoke, his voice stronger than I'd expected, stronger than mine certainly was.

Adolphe's intense gaze shifted from me to Souris. "What, Souris?" Gone was his light tone.

Souris slipped his arm from my loose grasp. He half-turned and stepped toward the table. "It has been a long night, I'm certain." He took another step away from me. "Surely a cup of tea would calm all our nerves."

Another step, and he was next to the table, right in front of his door.

"Souris, you bore me with your prattling. What, pray tell, makes you think I desire any tea?"

Adolphe's hand moved — just a little, but enough for me to react. I raised both of my hands up, and Adolphe's head twitched at my distraction.

Souris was as good as his word. From the corner of my eye, I watched him rush to his door, and it slammed behind him.

Adolphe's hard gaze didn't move at all. Souris wasn't his concern — his servant never had been. Adolphe was singularly focused on me.

As I hoped he would be.

"Stupid girl. You think a few years of study, limited by the resources I gave you, is enough to rise up against me? You think your beastly boy king will take you in now that he knows the truth?"

I froze, arm uplifted, the heat in my palms present and steady.

How did he know?

"You were a fool, you know," he continued as he reached into his flowing cape and withdrew the mirror — the one with the swirling face that showed more than any mirror should. My lips trembled as I wracked my brain to say something, anything.

"I had an idea you were sneaking about, especially once I brought the old book down. There are more books, you must know that. And you had to know that I'd never let you possess the ability to cure the king. Oh, my naïve Salome. But even I was surprised to see the wild animal welcome you with open arms and what I presume was a smile. Tell me, does he claim to love you? Does he tell that lie that so many tell to achieve their greatest desires?"

He's the one lying, I told myself. I wanted to close my ears to his harsh words, but the more he spoke, the sharper the words became until they were cutting at my heart.

"I knew how easy you were to manipulate. A few joy-infused words and you'd do anything anyone asked. What did he tell you? That you'd live with him? That he would take care of you?" Adolphe barked out a piercing laugh. "Oh, my pretty fool. Do you truly believe he'd take you in once he was a human king again, a beautiful man in his full glory and power?" Adolphe's eyes glanced at the mirror and back at me. "I couldn't believe it myself when I saw you with him. Even I couldn't believe you to be that gullible. But then, you learned the truth, didn't you, little girl? That once you didn't give him what he wanted, you were as useless to him as garbage, and he threw you out with it, didn't he?"

That grin on his face, a toothy, nightmarish grin, and I couldn't take it anymore. He may have seen me with Faustin, but he was so confident that he had put the mirror down when I left the castle. He hadn't seen what I did in the woods after. Adolphe didn't say it, but I could tell from his voice, from his stance, from his sheer audacity.

"And then to see him lift a mirror, so much like this one," he intoned as he waved the mirror in front of me. "A magic glass. My magic glass. You stole from me, yet again, little girl. And you gave that precious gift to a beast who turned you away."

He *had* watched the beast after I'd left the castle. He hadn't seen me in the woods. Or in the kitchens. He didn't know what I could do.

Worse, neither did I.

But I didn't care.

"I'm not a little girl," I said slowly, and unfurled my fingers.

The flames rushed from my hands in a huge blue and orange flare, snapping at Adolphe's robes so quickly he dropped the mirror. It clanged on the steps and broke, but he didn't notice that. He was too busy lifting his own hands.

Adolphe murmured under his breath. The flames stopped spreading, and he ducked away.

I grinned to myself.

He had to say the words to cast each of his spells. He wasn't as strong as I was. All I had to do was think them, and the world shifted at my command.

I curled my fingers around the flames like they were ropes, and with a rush of smugness, I whipped them around, snapping at his head and backside.

Adolphe screeched like a panicked child and tried to jump away, but his flowing cloak flicked against flames and ignited. He screamed and battered at the fiery cloak with his bare hands.

While he was occupied, I unleashed everything in the kitchens at him. Plates, cups, pans.

He curled into a ball, hiding beneath his cape, and I heard him chanting under his breath. I needed to stop that, so I flicked my fingers toward the hearth, and another fire roared to life. A snap of my wrist and the flames leapt out of the fireplace at Adolphe's unprotected backside and lit his cape on fire.

Adolphe screamed, forming random words, curses, spells, and the water pump roared to life, spraying him and extinguishing his cloak in a smoky cloud.

He rose, his legs shaking, and the water still spraying the kitchens and dousing his cloak. He wasn't taking any more chances with the fire. He gave me another horrifying grin, as if he knew something I didn't. My mind burned with a fever. He might have a trick up his sleeve, but then, so did I.

He didn't know that I had been sneaking into the study to read more of the book, that I had read all the spells and potions to the end.

Or that I had considered prudent to commit to memory. As he stood slowly, I waited, biding my time, baiting him, panting, pretending I was worn out. I wanted him to conjure up something dire, something ferocious, something that would keep me under his control forever. That was the spell I wanted him to force upon me.

The more dire, the better.

His mouth moved, speaking the words too low for me to hear. Then he lifted his hand and his face at the same time.

When he did, I put my arms in front of my chest, my hands cupped like I was trying to catch the water pouring from the pump. When his lips stopped moving, I chanted in my head: *This hand returns what is sent with ill intent. This hand returns to you the pain.*

Then I flicked my fingers out like I was flicking at an annoying bug.

I didn't know what to expect since I didn't know what spell he had cast, but I hadn't expected *that*.

As soon as my fingers flinched, a forceful rush of hot air blew away from me and at Adolphe. He began screaming, a crescendo scream that shook the stones and dislodged chunks of rock and debris. His hands, upraised a second ago, curled in on themselves, turning a pinkish white and shrinking. No, his whole body was shrinking, swallowing itself up and receding into his black cloak.

His screaming grew smaller as he shrunk, a decrescendo, and his arms disappeared under his cloak. His head followed until there was nothing on the ground but the black cloak itself. In a blink, he was gone.

My arms slumped against my sides, and I couldn't move. What had happened? Was he gone?

Had his spell been a disappearing spell of some sort?

I didn't know of any that existed and worked like this, but then, Adolphe had pointed out that there were more books in his study. I had much to learn, but disappeared?

Turning his spell on him took so much out of me, I swooned on my feet and braced my hands on my thighs for support. But it had worked! I had put my faith, and mine and Souris's future, into my hands and into that one spell, and it had worked!

I was still breathing hard when the door opened and Souris peeked out.

"What's happened, Salome?"

I pointed a weary, blistered finger at the cloak. "He's gone."

Souris shifted his bulging gaze to the charred-edged black heap on the floor, and his eyebrows rose.

"Are you sure?"

I spun my eyes to the cloak, and sure enough, it was moving. Only a little bit, but moving.

Oh, non!

Had I made a mistake? Was Adolphe coming back somehow?

I took a trepidatious step toward the cloak and reached down. It wasn't moving much, more like creeping. I lifted the edge of the cloak, trying to see in the dark shadows underneath.

I didn't see Adolphe, but that didn't mean he wasn't there.

Then a tiny nose peeked out from the shadow, its thin whiskers shaking as it sniffed. The nose was followed by a small body, a blackish-gray field mouse, not much larger than my thumb.

"What's that? A mouse?" Souris asked as he leaned farther out his door.

I whipped the cloak off the floor and tossed it into the fire at the hearth. The tiny mouse skittered across the stones toward the table. Souris leapt from his door and stamped his bare foot down in front of it. With a quick hand, he grabbed at the rodent's pink tail and lifted him. The suspended creature twirled and squeaked in protest.

"A mouse," Souris remarked with awe.

"He was going to turn *me* into a mouse?"

Souris looked from the mouse to me. "What? What do you mean?"

My own eyes were wide, my whole face a mask of surprise, I was certain. I moved closer to Souris to study the tiny creature protesting his suspended state. I poked its side, and it tried to bite me.

"The spell I cast," I explained, "was a powerful one that turns one's own evil, pain, curse, or the like back to them. He was casting me into a mouse, and I turned it on him. He turned himself into a mouse."

The animal squeaked again, as if it understood and complained that I had foiled his curse. The side of my mouth turned up slightly as we studied the wee thing.

"What do we do with it now?"

I glanced around the kitchens and found a giant glass canister with a cork lid. Grabbing a knife, I stabbed several holes into the lid, then brought the canister to Souris. He dropped the mouse into the canister. The mouse clawed at the smooth side as if to climb out but found no purchase. He slipped and slid around as I pushed the lid on tight.

I set the canister on the table and stepped back to stand next to Souris. We watched the panicked mouse scamper and claw, to no avail.

"We shall have to change your name, Souris," I told him.

He turned his head to me. The lines on his face had softened, still present, but not as deep or tight. He looked almost relaxed. "Why?"

"Well, we have a new *souris* now, a new mouse. And you should have a proper name since you are no longer a meek servant, don't you agree?"

His thin lips parted in his own side smile. "I always liked Pierre," he admitted.

I smiled. *A rock.* As he had always been my rock.

The perfect new name for him, indeed.

Chapter Fifteen

"What do we do now?" Souris, now Pierre, asked.

Truthfully, I had no idea. Adolphe had been the iron hand in the tower for so long. Now that he was, well, gone, what were Pierre and I to do?

I shrugged. "Do you want to leave here? It has so many bad memories. And I understand if you don't want to stay with me. With my horrid curses." I flicked my gaze to the mouse — the second person I had changed into an animal. *Mon Dieu!* How could Pierre want to stay with me, living with the threat of what might happen if I moved my fingers the wrong way?

Pierre dragged a wooden stool up against the table and sat wearily on it. This night had taken much out of my old friend, and it showed in his slumped shoulders and sallow skin. With a nervous gesture, he brushed his thin swatch of white hair across the pale dome of his head.

"Do you know how long I've been here, Salome?" he asked. He reached his arms across the table to take my hands in his. I shook my head. "Years, decades. Adolphe and I are old. Ancient. But I still would have left here with you when you asked earlier."

His voice was so patient, so tender after the horror of the night, my whole body trembled under his kind touch. I blinked to hold back tears that threatened to fall. I failed, and a matching set rolled slowly down my ash-covered cheeks.

"Why?" I whispered in a cry-ravaged tone. "Why would you do that?"

He patted my hand. "I told you earlier tonight that I'd go with you, that I'd do anything for you—"

"That was before I destroyed the kitchen and turned Adolphe into a mouse!" I cried.

Pierre pursed his lips at me before speaking again. "Well, that is true, but your tremendous ability doesn't change my heart. It takes so much more than that to sway one's heart from those they love. And if you still want to leave, you can, but I would go with you."

"You'd give up living here, in the tower, even if I left because I was afraid I might hurt you somehow? A place you've lived for so long and call home?"

He dipped his head to stare at the rough wooden tabletop.

"Sometimes we must give up what we want most in the world, what we think we want most in the world, to do the best thing for the ones we love. Even if I leave, where would I go? I love you, Salome, the daughter I never had, and I would never leave you. If you stay here, I stay here. If you leave, I'll go with you. That is what love is, Salome."

I moved to the other side of the table and wrapped my arms around Pierre's frail, slender shoulders. I loved him, too. He had made a home for me in this dark tower. He had been the father I had never had.

"So, we stay here? Live here as our own family? Can we do that?"

"I don't see why not? Nothing much will be different." Pierre pointed to the mouse scrambling around the glass jar. "With our new pet? Or will you release him?"

I leaned around Pierre and rested my chin on my palm as I studied the dark gray creature. It paused in its panicked scrambling and peered at me with its black eyes.

Adolphe's same black eyes in miniature. *Non,* I decided. So much at the tower would now be different.

"I think we should keep him as a pet, at least for a while. Just to make sure."

Pierre patted my free hand. "That's a sound idea. Now, we have a late night ahead of us, cleaning this mess. Unless you have a spell you can use to do that?"

I dropped my head and giggled under my breath. I was so tired. I wiggled my finger at him.

"I think my magic is done for the night. I'll get the broom."

I swept up the dirt and debris as Pierre put the dishes and the rest of the kitchen to rights. Adolphe's glass had fallen at the base of the stairs, glinting against the dim kitchen light. I lifted the gold frame off the ground, and it came up with half of the reflective surface remaining on the stones. The fractured shard was in one piece, and I tried to fit it into the glass frame. It fit, the huge break line scarring the surface. Would it still work? Might I fix or replace the glass, perhaps re-charm it?

The din of Pierre's busyness fell into the background as I stared into the broken glass, focusing my thoughts on Faustin so I might see what he was doing, if the mirror yet worked. The bottom part that hadn't fallen out of the frame swirled, and the image of Faustin appeared – of what I believed to be Faustin. The image was dark, no candlelight or fire to illuminate the king. Faustin was little more than a shadow in the night. He sat in the dark in a room that was not his study, and if I hadn't caught the glint of his eyes in the dark, I would have thought him asleep.

The poor beast. He, too, was having a most unpleasant night.

"Salome?" Pierre's voice tore me from my reverie. I turned to him.

He pointed to my lump of bedding tucked against the far side of the hearth. "You no longer have to sleep here. You can move into Adolphe's room. You are the mistress of this tower now, after all."

I shook my head. "*Non,* Pierre, we are the masters of this tower. You should take it for your old bones."

"I have a room," he said as he tilted his head toward his closet.

I reached for the table and set the glass down. "You should have a better place, a bigger place. Not a room off the kitchen."

Pierre leaned down and shook out my bedding. Ash and dust flew in the air.

"All those stairs?" he asked as he worked. "*Non, ma chou*. I had enough of that bringing Adolphe his meals each day. If you agree to come to the kitchens and take your meals with me, I will happily stay in that room. I have all I need."

"We will get you a better bed, nicer bedding. Whatever you need." I glanced up the stair where Adolphe's room was at the top of the tower. "But I don't think I can sleep up there tonight. It's so full of . . ." I hesitated, unsure of how I felt.

"Full of Adolphe?" Pierre finished for me, raising an eyebrow. I grinned sheepishly and nodded. "How about you sleep here tonight and tomorrow we will clean his room, remove his personal items, put on new bedding. Make the room yours."

Mine. How fine a word that was! I hadn't had my own space in this tower since Adolphe had relegated me here. Before that, it was an open part of the top of the tower, not a proper room with an actual bed. My heart leapt in my chest at the prospect of making this cold, grim tower a real home for the two of us.

Pierre finished fluffing my bedding for me. "Come. It's so late. Let's sleep, and tomorrow we can begin our new life together."

Those words – they wrapped me in a warm blanket of contentment, something I'd only experienced before at Faustin's study. Now, Pierre and I would have that here, together.

The words Pierre had spoken throughout the night rolled in my head and framed my dreams. I tossed and turned as my dreams showed me the darkened, lumbering figure of Faustin and echoed Pierre – *Sometimes we must give up what we want most in the world, what we think we want most in the world, to do the best thing for the ones we love . . .*

When I awoke in the morn, the sun had not fully kissed the horizon, and the kitchen was dim and quiet. My mind swirled with the memory of my dreams.

What I wanted most in the world was to be with Faustin. To love him and have him love me back.

But to do that would mean he would stay a beast forever, and being a beast weighed on him like a painful yoke, a tether that imprisoned him. As long as he remained cursed, he couldn't be the most Faustin, the fullness of the man or king in the beast form I loved.

The only way to break that curse was to find someone to love him, love him as deeply as I did – someone other than me.

That thought was a knife digging into my heart, twisting and turning until it rented and tore at the very fabric of my being.

How could I do that? Could I set my feelings aside and find someone else for him? Someone who might love him as much as I did? Someone he might love as much, or worse, more than me?

My body grew fevered at those thoughts, even as the cool stones and morning air pressed against me.

Yet, Pierre had said that he'd leave all he knew here at the tower, where he had spent most of his life, to come with me.

Could I do that same with Faustin? Give up everything I wanted, everything I desired, everything I knew about Faustin, to help him?

Then another thought came on the heels of that one, a thought that chilled me instantly — how could I *not*?

Before the Cursed Beast

What was the depth of my love if I didn't do anything and everything in my power to bring him back from his beastly state?

No matter what Adolphe had tried to insinuate the night before, Faustin would sacrifice all that for me. Maybe not now, but before last night, he would have — of that I was certain.

But the larger problem still loomed. If not me, if not *my* love, someone else had to fall in love with Faustin to break the curse. How was that going to happen when he was a horrendous, angry beast who lived in what amounted to a haunted castle that he didn't dare leave?

As I worked out the details of my new plan to break Faustin's curse, a tear slipped from the corner of my eye and trailed down my cheek. I wiped at it absently and threw off my covers. The stone floor was frigid against my bare feet.

The answer to my conundrum laid in Adolphe's study.

I grinned to myself as I grasped the broken magic glass and mounted the steps.

Non. Not Adolphe's study.

My study.

Chapter Sixteen

Once ensconced in the privacy of the study, I pulled the stool (Adolphe's stool, *non — my* stool) to the table. I tucked my cold feet under the hem of my thin shift and held the broken glass before me.

"Show me the beast," I commanded, and the larger bottom of the cracked face swirled to life.

The beast wasn't in his study – he hadn't appeared to have moved from the night before. Yet it was the break of morning, and though his thick curtains were closed, they were shorn and ripped, and pale sunlight slipped through every opening, basking the room in illuminating rays.

If possible, the bedchamber, for that's where he was, had been the focus of his anger even more than the study. Not a single piece of the room, from what I determined through the glass, was untouched. Papered wall, ripped. Curtains, torn and dangling precariously from their rods. Paintings and portraits were riddled with claw marks that ruined the beautiful images. His bedding in the background was also ripped to shreds, threads and feathers littering the floor. The destruction of the room also hadn't been cleaned up as had the study, apparently. Did he permit anyone in that room?

As for the beast, he snored in an overstuffed chair that had also been victimized by Faustin's razor-like claws. My chest thrummed and throbbed as I gazed at his sleeping face, one that should be peaceful in sleep yet managed to appear tight and angry while he dozed.

I moved my hand to set the mirror down when movement caught my eye. Faustin was waking.

I should put the glass down, I told myself. It was an invasion of his privacy to watch him thusly. That's what I told myself, but I was unable to tear my gaze from the swirling glass. Faustin rose wearily, groaning as he moved his burly girth. Then he stretched hugely – his paws threatened to brush the ornate ceiling – then threw open the door to his room. With a steady gait, one full of conviction, he turned to the right and mounted a series of steps that led to the third floor of the castle tower. He paused before a tall set of double doors, and I leaned into the mirror, intrigued. The doors appeared unmarked, unclawed, pristine, and completely unlike any other desecrated surface in the castle.

What room is this? Why is it untouched?

He shoved open the door, and the room was bathed in light so bright it nearly blinded me from this side of the glass. I squinted, desperate to see what this room was. My eyes adjusted, and I see the light came from stacked windows that reached from floor to ceiling on three sides of the room – east, west, and north – so the room always basked in natural sunlight.

And once I looked past the light, I understood why.

Books.

So many books.

I gasped.

I had heard of libraries such as this, but never had I seen one. We possessed few books at Adolphe's tower, and they were all magic books. My reading skills were passable enough to read those spells. To have access to so many books! Stories Adolphe had explained once and poo-pooed them as a waste of one's time – who needed such fairy stories? Fake stories of fake places and irritating characters, he'd commented with derision.

That so many books existed, so many tales and stories, fairy or not, sent a flare of pain through my head.

I hadn't known so many books existed in the world. And Faustin had them all in one room. Stacks upon stacks in bookshelves that put Adolphe's single meager bookshelf to shame. Polished to a burnished golden shine and embellished with elaborate carvings, Faustin's bookshelves reached the high tower ceiling, each completely filled with thick, leather bound, miraculous texts.

Had he read all those? Who might read all that?

What struck me the most was that this room was untouched by his furious hand. He hadn't taken his anger at his beastly state out on this room. Each book was neatly tucked on its beautiful shelf, ready for an interested reader to take down.

Why? Why this one room? I hadn't seen him read. I didn't recall many books in his study. Why so many stories? Had they belonged to his parents and he couldn't bear to destroy them? Had he –?

My eyes dropped from the glass to the table.

Non. Of course. He had an entirely other reason for keeping this room in such a fine state.

Stories and tales, they were an escape. A way to leave the manse, to engage with people, imaginary though they may have been, when he was stuck at the castle. A way to escape the present monstrous body he was stuck in.

As I returned my gaze to the glass, I watched as he moved from shelf to shelf, searching for something to help him escape the news I'd given him the night before.

He found a book, took it gently between two claws, and extracted it from the shelf. Then he settled onto a comfortable-looking blue chaise and opened the pages.

I set the mirror down and left him to his reading. I had encroached on him enough this morn.

Escape.

His actions got me thinking. I needed a way to break the curse, and I was sure that the secret was in finding someone to love him.

To love a beast? Maybe easy for me, because I saw the man he was before I cursed him, but to anyone else, he would appear as nothing more than an animal. It might take more than a love spell to make that happen.

Most love spells were made to unite one person to another, not a person to beast, after all.

But if I could use what I knew about Faustin, his gentleness, his strong presence, his love of books, to make someone fall in love with his nature if not his looks, then the spell might work. I'd have to tweak it and probably craft a potion to really make it work, and then, it would only be successful if I found the right person – an engaging young woman open to adventure, who didn't care about how someone looked, and who loved things like tea and books.

My head fell into my hands.

A lass who read? Most women might read at a basic level, but even if they did, most lasses weren't seeking adventure. They were looking for a handsome man who was strong and would marry them, giving them a life on a farm where they would raise babies who might do little more than farm and read at a basic level.

The odds were stacked against me.

I had one thing that worked in my favor. I hadn't fallen in love with Faustin until he was a beast.

And if I could do it, I was sure another person could as well.

I merely had to find the right woman.

At first, I considered telling Faustin. I thought that he if knew I'd found a solution, he might resume his enchanting manner and we could resume our friendship.

I quickly changed my mind. If I remained friends with him, I'd want something more. Then there was the jealousy. I couldn't bring myself to imagine Faustin loving someone else. Every time I thought about it, my chest clenched in on itself with a burning, throbbing ache.

So I didn't tell him. Better to sever the bond we'd had with that hard break than let it linger. Finding him a new love to heal his heart and his body was my only option.

I spent a few days redesigning my new bed chambers and studying with Pierre, whose entire visage had changed. The sallow, doughy appearance of his skin lessened, and pink roses bloomed in his cheeks. The shadows in his eyes disappeared, and like the rest of him, they sparkled under the newfound freedom of our tower.

The new bedding and bathing items in Pierre's small room had to help his health. Gone was the flat cot, and we'd replaced it with a fluffy down and straw mattress. I had also insisted that he take the thick blanket from Adolphe's bed after we had laundered it. Though it now smelled of fresh air and pine from drying on the line, it still reminded me too much of Adolphe, and my stomach roiled at the prospect of that bedding in my own chambers.

Pierre had no such compunctions. He spread the thickly quilted blanket on his bed and marveled at how far his room had come in so short a time.

"Like its master," I commented, giving his thin arm a light squeeze.

On the morning I decided to start searching for the young woman who would replace me in Faustin's heart (oh, the thought of it was a scorching dagger in my chest!), I put on my nicest kirtle and gown. Threadbare in some spots, it was still the finest I had, and given that the villages nearby weren't ones of wealth, the gown should help me blend in easily.

With a basket over my arm to complete my costume, I waved to Pierre and made my way to the woods.

I didn't take my regular trail toward the castle. Instead, I turned right. This path had a fork midway through the wood. I decided to take the northerly fork first and search there for my replacement.

Walking through the wood during the daytime was a uniquely beautiful experience. After traveling in the dark and shadows for so long, I experienced the brilliance of color and sound the woods offered during the day. The deep greens and browns, the leaves dancing overhead in the faint breeze, the tittering echo of delicate birds in the boughs all infused me with a lightness. I turned my face to the early autumn sun, letting the sunlight kiss my cheeks. When was the last time I had gone with Adolphe to the villages during the day? I couldn't recall.

The northerly village was the same one Adolphe and I had visited when I was a child. The apothecary was still there, the son most likely working the counter while his father, the apothecary I remembered, worked in the back where he sat and rested his curved back and legs. The small cafe sat on the corner of two streets, spilling heady and inviting scents of bread and chocolate onto the passersby. I shook my basket and heard the coins I had tucked away jingle. I hoped I had bought enough to pay for my pastry and hot chocolate. The mysteries of paying for goods was one thing Adolphe hadn't taught me.

While those familiar places called to me, they weren't the ones I was interested in. *Non*, I had a list in my head of what I was looking for in a woman, and that list dictated my destination.

At the far side of the main road, a squat building sat in the shadows of another larger one, tucked away and easily missed. I would have passed the building by if I hadn't been looking for it specifically.

I had never entered the bookshop before. The beast's library seemed important to him, so it made sense to me that I should find a woman who might also have an interest in books.

I mean, they should have something in common, shouldn't they? I wasn't an expert on relationships, given my limited social entanglements, but that made sense to me. Faustin's library was the sole room he hadn't destroyed, so the books or their contents must have held a measure of value to him. A woman who held the same values might be the right start.

A bell tinkled over my head when I opened the door. I glanced up at it, then at the elderly, rotund man who greeted me. His white mustache frolicked wildly atop his mouth when he smiled in my direction.

"Bonjour, mademoiselle!" His voice was jovial but not loud. Welcoming. "I haven't had the pleasure of seeing you in my shop before."

I stared at him for the moment it took me to realize he was asking me a question. My eyebrows flew high on my head. "Oh, *oui*! My name is Salome. This is my first time here."

His smile widened toward me. He spread his arms as wide as his girth allowed. "Well, then, welcome to Le Monde du Livres. The worlds of books, ready here for you. May I ask what interests you?"

My mouth froze part-way open. Interest? I had no idea what books might interest me! Other than magic books, and I couldn't very well tell him *that*.

"I don't have a preference today," I lied as soon as my tongue loosened. "May I look around at the different books?"

Was I permitted to do that? What if he said no? How would I watch the store for the ideal girl if not?

He gave me a half-bow, surprisingly with ease for such a round man, and held his hand toward the bookcases that crowded the shop.

"Please, take your time. Finding the perfect book is a process, and I want you to leave with the exact story for you."

I gave him a grateful smile and turned down the first row of towering bookcases. I didn't delve too far in – I wanted to keep an eye on who entered the shop – but the myriad of leathery book spines splayed with rich, jewel-toned colors kept my rapt attention.

So many books! How did one decide? And my exact story? Unless the store had a book where a mysterious, outcast girl fell in love with a beast that she had cursed, and they lived happily ever after, then I didn't want any of the books.

The bell tinkled, and I stilled. I held one of the precious tomes in my hands, pretending to look through it as I lifted my hooded gaze to the door. An older man, not as old as the shopkeeper, with graying hair. Nope, not him. I went back to flipping through the book.

That happened several times, and after an hour, I was starting to lose hope. I had considered that the shopkeeper might tell me it was time to leave, but all he did was ask if I had found anything and offer up the next row of bookshelves to help me on my quest.

I had moved to the middle section of bookshelves and held a book about an old king of the desert with a name I couldn't pronounce when the door chimed again. I barely lifted my eyes, expecting yet another older man, when I stilled.

The book I held slipped from my fingers and slammed against the hardwood floor. The shopkeeper peeked down my aisle. "Need help?"

"*Non*, my apologies. It slipped from my fingers."

Another wide, honest smile. "Well, then, keep looking! I know what you seek is here."

You have no idea, I thought as he turned toward the young woman who had entered the store.

Pretending to be deeply engrossed in the information about the king, I shifted closer to the edge of the bookcase and watched the woman who spoke in an animated manner with the shopkeeper.

She was pretty, not stunning like I'd seen in some of the portraits at Faustin's castle, but with a delicate beauty that transcended anything I had seen in this village. Fair skin, eyes like alder tree bark, and her thick walnut hair pulled back loosely. When she walked, she favored her toes, so it didn't appear that she was walking at all, rather floating. But it was her voice, the excitement in her voice when she spoke to the shopkeeper, that caught my attention the most.

"Thank you for lending me this book!"

"You enjoyed it then?" The shopkeeper's jovial tone matched hers.

"Oh yes! Magic beans and an ogre! It was wonderful! Thank you for lending it to me."

Lending? She didn't buy the book? Did she not love the books? Was I mistaken about this young woman?

"Of course! But you finished it so quickly! Are you here for another book? I don't have anything new."

Non, nothing new. Most of the books I had pulled off the shelves wore a layer of dust atop their pages. This thick desert king one in particular. I wasn't surprised – the book didn't seem engaging in the least. Rather dry. And I don't think it contained any information about magic beans. Now *that* book sounded interesting.

"Then I'll take this one, if I may?"

"Again? You've read it so many times already."

The shopkeeper's eyes drifted to me, and I dropped my gaze to the thin pages of the book I held.

"Then if you love it so much, you should keep it."

I lifted my eyes again to see him and the young woman in a blue dress. Her entire being seemed to shimmer at the gift.

"But I can't pay you!"

Oh, and she was humble as well. The girl was getting better and better.

"Your exuberance over the book is payment enough for me. Here, I'll wrap it for you."

"No need!" the girl told him. "I'll read it now!"

The shopkeeper laughed as he handed over the book. The girl, true to her word, immediately opened the book and started reading as she left the shop. She stopped at the door.

"Good day to you, Maurice, and thank you!"

"You are welcome, Belle. Good day to you."

Belle. That was her name. It fit – she was a pretty woman in so many different ways.

She waved over her head as she left the shop, the chime of the bell announcing her exit. The brightness she'd brought into the shop departed with her.

Was it possible? Had I found the exact woman already?

I snapped my book shut and replaced it on the shelf. Then I approached the shopkeeper. He lifted his head and smiled at me again. Did he know how disarming his smile was? *Oui*, he had to.

"Did you find the story you were looking for?"

I shook my head. "*Non*, but the girl who was just here, she had a book about magic beans?"

His bushy white eyebrows lifted on his face. "*Oui*! It is here. Are you interested in it?"

He placed the book on the table in front of him and patted it. With a tentative hand, I opened the cover, studying the title. It was about a boy named Jack, from what I could tell.

"Yes, I would like to purchase the book," I told him. Maybe I would learn more about the girl from what she read.

"Excellent. I'll wrap this up for you." He gently pulled the book from my fingers and placed it on top of thin, brown paper.

"It was a kind thing you did for that girl. The book?" I raised one eyebrow in question, hoping he'd take the bait.

"For Belle? Oh yes. She loves to read, and if she had to buy her books to have enough, well, that wouldn't happen. A kinder, gentler girl I've never met. You can judge a person by the books they read, *oui*?" he asked with a knowing look. Was he trying to judge me? Well, Belle had read the book . . .

"What does this book say about a person, then?" I asked, pointing at my package.

He lifted it up to his eye level, studying the wrapped book as if the answer was printed on the plain paper.

"A person who reads this story, and others like it, has a vast imagination, a flair for the dramatic, and cheers for the character who never seems to win. Then they celebrate in the character's success, even if it means nothing for them." He gave me a side look. "Does that describe you?"

"I don't really know," I answered honestly. "But if that is the type of person who reads this book, then I should probably read it so I can be that type of person. Right?"

He grinned knowingly and held the book to me. "You can be any type of person you desire to be. The book costs five *sous*."

I slipped the package into my basket and retrieved the velvet sack that held my coins. Which one was a *sou*? Would I have still have enough for the pastry after? My hand shook as I studied the coins in my palm.

The shopkeeper didn't change his smile. He reached over the table and poked around in my palm, found the coins he had requested, and closed my fingers on the rest. His earnest nature spoke to me, and I took a risk.

"*Monsieur*, might I ask you a question about these coins?"

He lifted his sparkling eyes to mine. "Of course, my dear. Any question you have."

I opened my fingers and exposed the coins to him again. "Do I still have enough for a pastry and hot chocolate at the shop down the street?"

His rotund belly shook with his gentle laugh and he pointed to the coins in my hand, assuring me that I did indeed have enough.

I thanked him as I left, not sure if I thanked him for his help with the book, with the coins, or, without his knowledge, the girl.

I returned to the village several times, basket in hand, watching for the girl. While she had initially appeared to be the exact person I was searching for, I wanted to make sure.

Non, I reprimanded myself. *You are biding your time.*

And that was true. I was delaying making up my mind because if she was the woman I selected, that meant she'd find herself in Faustin's arms too soon. My lesser nature wanted to delay that inevitability as long as possible.

But it did nothing good for Faustin to make him wait, and in the end, the need to break the curse was more important than my petty jealousies.

The last time I was in the village, I made sure to clip a fine red rose from the bushes growing near the benches. A plan formed in my head for the rose, which I would charm specifically for him. I then spent the afternoon crafting the perfect spell and potion that would lead to Faustin's release from his beastly prison. Once everything was ready, I returned to the village.

While I was in the village watching her, I brought my book and sat on a bench, reading it as best I could. The book was more humorous than not, and by the time I finished it, I decided I had enjoyed the story of a giant beanstalk more than I initially believed I would. I put it on one of the shelves in my study, right next to my magic books, which contained spells and potions that really could make a stalk grow that tall. I didn't believe I would find any golden geese at the top, though.

I came upon the girl one sunny afternoon when I had the spell and potion prepared. She had selected a loaf of day-old break from the baker, the same place where I indulged my pastry craving, and stepped out into the busy street. I had intentionally selected this day, this moment, because of how busy it was.

If she noticed me bumping into her or blowing my dusty concoction into her face, she didn't let on. She wiped absently at her face, as if brushing loose dirt from her cheeks, and carried on down the street in her oddly light way of walking.

Now all I had to do was let the beast know my plan so he was prepared when she arrived.

Chapter Seventeen

My heart raced in my chest faster than my feet pounded the ground as I ran down the trail. Instead of going home to my tower, I passed it and headed for Faustin's castle. It was daytime, and I briefly wondered what he would make of my daytime visit. All my previous visits had been nocturnal visits to hide our encounters from Adolphe. The liberty of going to see Faustin during daylight added to my light-headedness.

The wind kicked up, a cooler wind announcing that autumn was slowly closing her grasp on the land. Soon the leaves would fall from the trees and snow would blanket the earth. Will the girl have encountered Faustin by then? Might his curse be broken by winter?

While my hopes were high, the reality, I realized, was quite different. I may have fallen in love with the beast in a season, but I had known what he looked like before his transformation and commiserated with him over his misfortune. That was an attachment we shared before anything else.

This new girl, she would have to fall in love with Faustin as a beast. Was my magic strong enough for that? Would it happen in time with the charmed rose as I had planned? More weights to drag down my hopes.

I scrambled past the overgrowth at the gate – it had been weeks since I had last visited, and apparently no one kept up the wall line. The small yard opened before me, leading to the stained-glass window.

At night, it was easier to see Faustin through the window when the fire lighted the room, and the night where I stood was dark. At night, I could see him plainly. In the daytime, however, the sun's rays reflected off the multicolored window, casting the room in a hazy blur of color.

I couldn't see if Faustin was in the study or not.

Pressing my nose, I tried to see inside. What if he wasn't in the study? What if I had to search him out in his castle? Other than watching from the mirror, I hadn't actually been in any other rooms. How might I find him?

A shadow moved across the window, and I lurched back as the door swung open.

"What are you doing here?" Faustin growled at me.

Oh, my poor Faustin. He appeared so worse for wear. Hopelessness washed over him, making his eyes droop and his wild fur lusterless. His normally tall and broad shoulders sloped, so his face hung low. It was like he carried his despondency across his shoulders in a suffocating yoke, and I had to steel myself lest I began crying.

I held out my hand in supplication. He might despise me, but I still loved him so much.

"Please, Faustin. Might I speak with you?"

He crossed his thick arms across this chest.

"Why? About what?"

"About your –" I waved my hand from his furry head to his large, bear-like feet.

"My what? My hideous form that you changed me into? My horrible curse you promised to break and then said you wouldn't?"

I lifted one finger to him, like I would a child. "*Non,* those words never left my lips. I said I *couldn't.* There's a difference. Please, let me come in so we might speak."

He stared at me for the space of several heartbeats, and as I watched, some of the sparkle returned to his eyes. So he wasn't completely forlorn yet.

Faustin grunted and retreated into his study, leaving the door open. Presuming I was supposed to follow, I stepped into the study.

Though it didn't necessarily look worse than the last time I'd been his guest, the ragged hearthstones looked more abused, and the scratches extended across the stone and swept over the delicate cream wallpaper, leaving it in ribbons.

He didn't gesture to a seat or face me. He turned to the hearth, giving me his back, and waited for me to speak. I stood behind him and stared at the cold hearth just past his body.

"I've come up with a solution, Faustin. A possible way to break the curse."

His upper body shifted a bit, as if to peer at me from the side of his eyes, but that was all he did. I was rather surprised the movement didn't come with a derisive snort.

"I can't fix you," I continued. "That is, *I* can't be the one to change you back, but the spell has a loophole, if you will."

This time he whirled at me, glaring, his blue eyes narrow and full of distrust, his thick, furry brow low.

"A loophole? What is it this time? Another false promise?"

His voice was so ragged, I cowered back away from him. Then I nodded, and from under my cape, I removed the rose I had charmed. It was designed to work in tandem with the young girl from the village, Belle, to break his curse. The one thing I couldn't do. The one thing that had turned him from me.

His heart might be hardened with hatred at my apparent treachery, but mine was not. I had fallen in love with the man under the beast's skin, and I'd not rob him of his future because of how he felt. His hatred of me didn't mean I loved him any less.

And if this plan with Belle was the solution, though it pained everything in my being, I would make sure it worked so he could be the human king he so desired to be again.

"What is this? A rose is going to save me? Break the curse?" Cynical disbelief dripped from his slippery beast lips. He spoke as though I was touched in the head.

"This rose, it's more like an hourglass. It will mark the amount of time before you become human again." I stepped to the table and set it down, only it didn't fall to its side, bloom-heavy, like other flowers did. Rather, it stood on its stem upright, as though it yet grew on the bush.

Faustin pushed himself off the hearth and stood by my side at the table. The hard anger of his face settled into an expression of surprised awe at the upright rose before him. He reached out a claw and brushed gently at a petal, testing to see if the magical bloom was real.

"This rose breaks the curse?" His growling had also toned down, nearly back to his steady, deep rumble.

"Of a sort," I told him.

I kept my eyes on the rose, for I couldn't look at his face with what I had to tell him next. Otherwise, I would start crying, I was sure of it. My head may have known what was needed and was prepared for it, but my heart wasn't on board.

"What else?" he asked.

I took a deep breath to still my shaking nerves.

"When I said I couldn't change you, the reason for that is the spell itself. As I told you before, the person who casts the curse can't undo it. That was one of the reasons Adolphe had me curse you. If he had done cast the curse upon you, then I could have easily changed you back."

"But since you cast the spell," he spoke slowly. I nodded.

"I couldn't break the curse."

"Mmm," he mumbled, as if really understanding why he was yet a beast for the first time. The knowledge was finally able to permeate his anger. Time had given him the gift of perspective, tempering his anger at my previous confession.

"I didn't know that part of the curse when I first promised you that I would break it. I didn't know until Adolphe brought down the ancient text, and I read the spell myself for the first time."

"He finally let you read it?" Faustin paused, then his eyes widened. "Wait, why are you here during the day?"

Ahh, he noticed. I had wondered if he'd notice my daytime visit and would ask about it. I hadn't yet decided how much to tell him, but honesty hadn't led me wrong yet.

"I fought with Adolphe the night I came back from your castle. And I won that fight. Adolphe no longer has control over me. I am my own woman now, my own magician. The tower and all the magic books are mine. So I had time to study and find this solution. That's why I'm here."

I didn't mention that Adolphe was also now a mouse. It wasn't a lie, more of an omission.

"The flower isn't the solution?" He moved closer to me, and I froze.

Don't come closer, I said to myself. *Don't lean into me, want to touch me. It will only make this more difficult.*

I shifted to the side, as if to give him more access to the upright rose.

"It's like a countdown. *Non*, the solution is something far greater." I swallowed, and while I paused, Faustin took my hand in his paw.

Non, non, non! I shouted in my head. I tried to pull my hand away, but his grip was too tight.

"Wait, Salome. You said that all I needed to break the curse was for someone to love me. But you love me and that doesn't break the curse. Was there another way to break it?"

The tenderness in his voice pulled on my heart like the loose threads of a woolen cloak unraveling, drawing out long and shredding the remains of my heart. I swallowed hard, trying to find the right words.

"That's just it, Faustin. The solution is the same. Only, I can't be the one to love you. Someone else has to. Now, I already found someone —"

"What? *Non!* I love you. I don't want anyone else's love." He didn't roar, but it was building, and I braced myself.

I lifted my chin so my face was close to his. "*Non*, Faustin, but you need someone else's love. This girl, she is perfect for you, I believe. She is pretty, very pretty, with a smart character. And she —"

"*Non*! Salome!" He gripped my hands so tight, I feared he didn't know his strength and would break the fine bones of my fingers. "I don't want her. I want you!"

That was it. The final straw. The tears broke free and flooded my eyes, staining my cheeks as they fell to my kirtle. I choked back a wet sob.

"Don't say that anymore, Faustin. This is how it must be. For you to be the king you should, to be the man you want, *this* is how it must be. She likes to read. She's friendly, and she isn't looking for wealth or power. She seems to desire an adventure, and meeting you would be an adventure indeed."

The words poured out of my mouth as hard and fast as the tears fell from my eyes.

Faustin didn't want to hear it. His head shook back and forth in a steady movement, his eyes wide.

"Non, Salome. I told you, non! We will find another way. We can wait. I can wait. This isn't so –"

"Don't say it, Faustin." I managed to wrest my hand from his paw and cupped his furry cheek. "You need to be king, Faustin. A real king. You need to be a man. To live as fully as a man can. I love you too much to keep you cursed in this form. And if it means walking away from you so you might find love with someone else, though it slays my heart, I will do it."

His head shook against my hand. "*Non,* Salome," he rasped.

"I will do it," I promised.

Then I kissed him, the thin, leathery line of his lips, the fur surrounding them tickling my face. His arms went around me, crushing me to him, and that low growl resumed in his chest, rumbled through my mouth and down to the center of my being.

He was everything, and the only thing, in the world I wanted.

The only thing I couldn't have.

I quickly turned from Faustin and gestured toward the rose. It was more than a measurement of time for him – it had one more charm to help make sure the curse would break. For this girl, Belle, wouldn't love him if he couldn't love her back. I needed him to forget about me.

"Before I leave, you must touch this thorn," I instructed. His bushy eyebrows dropped low on his forehead, but he peered down to where I pointed. "The rose is charmed, but it is charmed to do one more thing. To make sure this all works, you must forget about me, Faustin. Prick your paw on the thorn, and I will be wiped from your memory."

He opened his mouth to protest once more. I pressed my palm gently to his jaw to close it.

His happiness, his ability to live a full life was more important than me or my love for him. I pressed my hands against his chest and pushed away. He stood by the rose with his arms upraised, as if ready to embrace me again. I hurried to the still open door.

"Don't follow me, Faustin. Know this. I love you enough to let you go. This way we can both do what we are supposed to. The girl will arrive soon. Her name is Belle. Convince her to stay, show her the affection I know you can, and by the time the last petal of the rose falls, you will be human again. Now, touch the thorn."

I made to exit, reaching the step outside the door, then paused. I looked past the doorway to the broken, sobbing beast. He appeared worse now than when I'd arrived. Everything inside me longed to race to him, to embrace him, to tell him I would love him as a beast no matter what.

But as I'd said, I wasn't a liar. And I had told him I loved him enough to let him go. So I would. I waited by the door until he touched the thorn as I had bid. A crimson drop of blood welled on his paw. It was done.

"Forget about me, Faustin, and love this girl." Then I lowered my voice. "But I will always love you."

I turned and raced out the door and into the woods before he could follow. Not that he would. He was forgetting me the moment I left.

My feet where heavy but my mind was light. I had done the right thing, and now the beast, the man, the king I loved would have everything he needed in this world to be the finest king and best man he could.

And though my heart wrenched when I thought of him and Belle, I made my way back to the tower, ready to do everything I needed to be the best magician possible. My knowledge of who I was and what I could do hardened my heart as I strode home.

I would never have the love I craved with Faustin. But what I possessed was far greater, and I would throw myself into it. Magic would be my love.

Because you never know who might need my magic touch one day.

The End

Before the Cursed Beast

If you love this book, be sure to leave a review! Reviews are life blood for authors, and I appreciate every review I receive!

Love what you read? Want more from Michelle? Click the image below to receive Gavin, the free Glen Highland Romance short ebook, free books, updates, and more in your inbox.

Get your free copy by signing up for my newsletter at linktr.ee/mddalrympleauthor

Before the Cursed Beast

Look for *Before the Red Cloak,* coming soon!

Fairy Tale Notes

Beauty and the Beast is one of my favorite fairy tales, especially the Disney version. A girl who reads and falls in love a giant, scary beast of a man? Oh, swoon.

But to turn someone into a beast for the slight sin of not giving shelter for the night? To me, it seemed like there had to be something more going on.

So I wrote it.

The old woman who cursed the king isn't really seen at the villain, but in my head, she should be. She's the reason for the entire story, the origin event. Then I have to ask myself – why did she do that? Those are the stories I love to read. It's like a sneak peek into a different world, one outside the story, delving into the characters in such a way as to make them richer, to make us care about them more.

As I've mentioned before, I've always been a fan of the villains in our favorite fairy tales. I even owned a Disneyland sweatshirt at one point – a

Villains sweatshirt. I wonder what happened to that shirt?

So I just have to come up with a backstory for all these villains. Or the secondary character who just don't get their stories told.

These stories are a move away from my usual historical romances. They are not as entrenched in history; they are a bit darker; and the don't necessarily end in the traditional Happily Ever After (gasp!). In this series, I tried to imagine, what would it be like for those villains before they were painted as a villain. Are they really as evil as they are shown in the princess story? What if I were in their shoes – what would I have done? Would the outcome have been any different? Could I have been painted as the villain then?

Oh, what might have happened! This series delves into those complex ideas, that maybe our villains aren't the villain we believe them to be.

I hope you enjoy these backstories as much as I do.

A Thank You–

Thank you to my loyal readers – for you I am eternally grateful. Thank you for trying something a bit different from me.

To my kids and family, thank you for always supporting me. Even though writing takes me away from them, or I drive them nuts talking bookshop, they are my best cheerleaders. I couldn't do this without their support.

I need to give a special thanks to my 22-year-old who is also a beta reader, and my hubby, who is also my first reader.

My invaluable proofreader, Lizzie with Phoenix Book Promotion, who can read my writing in such a way to polish it beautifully, I also owe a huge thank you!

Finally, and just as eternally, I need to thank Michael, the man in my life who has been so supportive of my career shift to focus more on writing, and who makes a great sounding board for ideas. Thank you, babe, for putting up with this and for keeping me from being a villain and for giving me and the kids our own Happily Ever After.

About the Author

Michelle Deerwester-Dalrymple is a professor of writing and an author. She started reading when she was 3 years old, writing when she was 4, and published her first poem at age 16. She has written articles and essays on a variety of topics, including several texts on writing for middle and high school students. She has written fifteen books under a variety of pen names and is also slowly working on a novel inspired by actual events. She lives in California with her family of seven.

Find Michelle on your favorite social media sites, all her books, and sign up for her newsletter here:
https://linktr.ee/mddalrympleauthor

Before the Cursed Beast

Also by the Author:

Glen Highland Romance

The Courtship of the Glen –Prequel Short Novella
To Dance in the Glen – Book 1
The Lady of the Glen – Book 2
The Exile of the Glen – Book 3
The Jewel of the Glen – Book 4
The Seduction of the Glen – Book 5
The Warrior of the Glen – Book 6
An Echo in the Glen – Book 7
The Blackguard of the Glen – Book 8

The Celtic Highland Maidens

The Maiden of the Storm
The Maiden of the Grove
The Maiden of the Celts
The Roman of the North
The Maiden of the Stones – coming soon
The Maiden of the Loch – coming soon

The *Before* Series

Before the Glass Slipper
Before the Magic Mirror
Before the Cursed Beast
Before the Red Cloak – coming soon

Before the Magic Lamp

Glen Coe Highlanders
Highland Burn – coming soon

Historical Fevered Series – short and steamy romance
The Highlander's Scarred Heart
The Highlander's Legacy
The Highlander's Return
Her Knight's Second Chance
The Highlander's Vow
Her Outlaw Highlander
Her Knight's Christmas Gift

As M. D. Dalrymple: Men in Uniform Series
Night Shift – Book 1
Day Shift – Book 2
Overtime – Book 3
Holiday Pay – Book 4
School Resource Officer -- Book 5
Undercover – Book 6 coming soon

Before the Cursed Beast

Campus Heat Series
Charming – Book 1
Tempting – Book 2
Infatuated – Book 3
Craving – Book 4
Alluring – Book 5 -- coming soon

Printed in Great Britain
by Amazon